# LYING
# CHEATING &
# STEALING

# LYING CHEATING & STEALING

Great writers on getting what you want
when you want it

Edited by Sara Nicklès

CHRONICLE BOOKS

SAN FRANCISCO

For John Strom, Jr.,
the most honest man I know.

# CONTENTS

I am not a crook.

—RICHARD NIXON

# INTRODUCTION

## Sara Nicklès

WE ALL DO IT: STEALING OFFICE SUPPLIES, A FIB ABOUT OUR weight on the driver's license, locker room boasts, cosmetic surgery, the embellished resumé. Why do we do it? The justifications are as numerous as the lies. But there is no denying that certain thrill when we've gotten away with something, even temporarily. It's one of a child's first natural inclinations. It's the inspiration for most country and western songs. It's the age-old foundation of politics.

The truth is, we all have different standards for what passes as honesty. From faking an orgasm to fixing the World Series, who is to judge which is the more serious crime? In this anthology, we leave that judgment to some of the best American writers of the twentieth century—for who has more experience in fabrication than those who tread the fine line between fiction and nonfiction?

We have Alexander Woollcott's creative solution to losing at the roulette wheel; James Thurber's wry account of an embezzler he once knew; Kate Chopin's wistful remembrance of a past dalliance; and Russell Baker's, Mary Karr's, Geoffrey Wolff's, and Russell Banks's versions of the tall tales they were told in childhood. The song "Frankie and Johnny" provides the blunt justification for a fatal shot, "He was her man, but he done her wrong," while Cynthia Heimel offers a distinctly more poetic view of adultery when she observes, "Infidelity is such a pretty word, so light and delicate."

So let us tip our hats for a moment to the cat burglars, plagiarists, impostors, con artists, and counterfeiters out there. For those of us for whom crossing the line means taking an extra newspaper from the vending machine, this rich catalogue of roguery provides illicit delights without any of the unpleasant consequences—akin to lusting in our hearts. We'll let these writers take the risk for us as they variously observe, sometimes shake their heads over, perhaps deplore, yet ultimately savor these guilty pleasures.

# CONFESSIONS OF A BURGLAR

## Woody Allen

*(Following are excerpts from the soon to be published memoirs of Virgil Ives, who is currently serving the first of four consecutive ninety-nine-year sentences for various felonies. Mr. Ives plans on working with children when he gets out.)*

SURE I STOLE. WHY NOT? WHERE I GREW UP, YOU HAD TO steal to eat. Then you had to steal to tip. Lots of guys stole fifteen per cent, but I always stole twenty, which made me a big favorite among the waiters. On the way home from a heist, I'd steal some pajamas to sleep in. Or if it was a hot night, I'd steal underwear. It was a way of life. I had a bad upbringing, you might say. My dad was always on the run from the cops and I never saw him out of disguise till I was twenty-two. For years, I thought he was a short, bearded man with dark glasses and a limp; actually, he was tall and blond and resembled Lindbergh. He was a professional bank robber, but sixty-five was the mandatory retirement age, so he had to get out. Spent his last few years in mail fraud, but the postal rates went up and he lost everything.

Mom was wanted, too. Of course in those days it wasn't the way it is now, with women demanding equal rights, and all. Back then, if a woman turned to crime the only opportunities open to her were blackmail and, once in a while, arson. Women were used in Chicago to drive getaway cars, but only during the drivers' strike, in 1926. Terrible strike. It lasted eight weeks, and whenever a gang pulled a job and ran out with the money they were forced to walk or take a cab.

I had a sister and two brothers. Jenny married money. Not an actual human being—it was a pile of singles. My brother Vic got in with a gang of plagiarists. He was in the middle of signing his name to "The Waste Land" when the feds surrounded the house. He got ten years. Some rich kid from a highfalutin family who signed Pound's "Cantos" got off on probation. That's the law for you. Charlie—that's my youngest brother—he's been a numbers runner, a fence, and a loan shark. Never could find himself. Eventually he was arrested for loitering. He loitered for seven years, till he realized it was not the kind of crime that brought in any money.

The first thing I ever stole was a loaf of bread. I was working for Rifkin's Bakery, where my job was to remove the jelly from doughnuts that had gone stale and transfer it to fresh goods. It was very exacting work, done with a rubber tube and a scalpel. If your hands shook, the jelly went on the floor and old man Rifkin would pull your hair. Arnold Rothstein, who we all looked up to, came in one day and said he wanted to get his hands on a loaf of bread but he absolutely refused to pay for it. He hinted that this was a chance for some smart kid to get into the rackets. I took that as a cue, and each day when I left I put one slice of rye under my coat, until after three weeks I had accumulated a whole loaf. On the way to Rothstein's office, I began to feel remorse, because even though I hated Rifkin his wife had once let me take home two seeds from a roll when my uncle was dying. I tried to return the bread, but I got caught while I was trying to figure out which loaf each slice belonged to. The next thing I knew, I was in Elmira Reformatory.

Elmira was a tough joint. I escaped five times. Once I tried to sneak out in the back of a laundry truck. The guards got suspicious, and one of them poked me with his stick and asked me what the hell I was doing lying around in a hamper. I looked him right in the eye and said, "I'm some shirts." I could tell he was dubious. He kept pacing back and forth and staring at me. I guess I got a little panicky. "I'm some *shirts*," I told him. "Some denim work shirts—blue ones." Before I could say another word, my arms and legs were manacled and I was back in stir.

I learned everything I knew about crime at Elmira: how to pick pockets, how to crack a safe, how to cut glass—all the fine points of the trade. For instance, I learned (and not even all professional criminals know this) that in the event of a shootout with the cops, the cops are always allowed the first two shots. It's just the way it's done. Then you return fire. And if a cop says, "We have the house surrounded, come out with your hands up," you don't just shoot wildly. You say, "I'd prefer not to," or "I'd rather not at this particular time." There's a right way to do these things, but today . . . Well, why go into all that?

For the next few years of my life I was the best damn burglar you ever saw. People talk about Raffles, but Raffles had his style and I had mine. I had lunch with Raffles' son once. Nice guy. We ate at the old Lindy's. He stole the pepper mill. I stole the silverware and napkins. Then he took the ketchup bottle. I took his hat. He got my umbrella and tiepin. When we left we kidnapped a waiter. It was quite a haul. The original Raffles began as a cat burglar. (I couldn't do that, because the whiskers make me sneeze.) He'd dress up in this beat-up cat suit and dart over rooftops. In the end, he was caught by two dogs from Scotland Yard dressed as dogs. I suppose you've heard of the Kissing Bandit? He'd break into a joint and rob the victim, and if it was a woman he'd kiss her. It was sad the way the law finally nailed him. He had two old dowagers tied up and he was prancing in front of them singing "Gimme a Little Kiss, Will Ya, Huh?" when he slipped on a footstool and fractured his pelvis.

Those boys made all the headlines, but I pulled off some capers that the police never did figure out. Once, I entered a mansion, blew the safe, and removed six thousand dollars while a couple slept in the same room. The husband woke up when the dynamite went off, but when I assured him that the entire proceeds would go to the Boys' Clubs of America he went back to sleep. Cleverly, I left behind some fingerprints of Franklin D. Roosevelt, who was President then. Another time, at a big diplomatic cocktail party, I stole a woman's diamond necklace while we were shaking hands. Used a vacuum cleaner on her—an old Hoover. Got her necklace and earrings. Later, when I opened the bag I found some false teeth there, which belonged to the Dutch Ambassador.

My most beautiful job, though, was when I broke into the British Museum. I knew that the entire floor of the Rare Gems Room was wired and the slightest pressure on it would set off an alarm. I was lowered in upside down by a rope from the skylight, so I wouldn't touch the ground. I came through neat as you please, and in a minute I was hovering over the famous Kittridge Diamonds in their display case. As I pulled out my glass cutter a little sparrow flew in through the skylight and landed on the floor. The alarm sounded and eight squad cars arrived. I got ten years. The sparrow got twenty to life. The bird was out in six months, on probation. A year later, he was picked up in Fort Worth for pecking Rabbi Morris Klugfein into a state of semiconsciousness.

What advice would I give the average homeowner to protect himself against burglars? Well, the first thing is to keep a light on in the house when you go out. It must be at least a sixty-watt blub; anything less and the burglar will ransack the house, out of contempt for the wattage. Another good idea is to keep a dog, but this is not foolproof. Whenever I was about to rob a house with a dog in it, I threw in some dog food mixed with Seconal. If that didn't work, I'd grind up equal parts of chopped meat and a novel by Theodore Dreiser. If it happens that you are going out of town and must leave your house unguarded, it's a good idea to put a cardboard silhouette of yourself in the window. Any silhouette will do. A Bronx man once placed a cardboard silhouette of Montgomery Clift in his window and then went to Kutsher's for the weekend. Later, Montgomery Clift himself happened to walk by and saw the silhouette, which caused him great anxiety. He attempted to strike up a conversation, and when it failed to answer for seven hours Clift returned to California and told his friends that New Yorkers were snobbish.

If you surprise an intruder in the act of burglarizing your home, do not panic. Remember, he is as frightened as you are. One good device is to rob *him*. Seize the initiative and relieve the burglar of his watch and wallet. Then he can get into your bed while you make a getaway. Trapped by this defense, I once wound up living in Des Moines for six years with another man's wife and three children, and only left when I was fortunate enough to surprise another burglar, who took my place. The six years I lived with that family were very happy ones, and I often look back on them with affection, although there is also much to be said for working on a chain gang.

[1980]

17

# RIEN NE VA PLUS

## Alexander Woollcott

WE WERE SITTING UNDER THE MIDSUMMER STARS AT MONTE Carlo, eating a soufflé and talking about suicide, when a passing newsmonger stopped at our table all aglow with the tidings that that young American with the white forelock had just been found crumpled on the beach, a bullet-hole in his heart. Earlier in the evening—it was shortly before we came out of the Casino in quest of dinner—we had all seen him wiped out by a final disastrous turn of the wheel. And now he lay dead on the shore.

I shall have to admit that the news gave a fillip to the occasion. It came towards the end of a long, luscious dinner on the terrace opposite the Casino. We were a casually assembled carful, who had driven over from Antibes in the late afternoon, planning to play a little roulette as an appetizer and then to dine interminably.

When we had arrived in the *Salles Privées* a few hours before, there was only standing room around our table at first. In this rapt fringe, I encountered Sam Fletcher, a dawdling journalist who lived on occasional assignments from the Paris offices of American newspapers. He pointed out the notables to me. There was Mary Garden, for instance, playing intently, losing and winning, losing and winning, with that economy of emotional expenditure which one usually reserves for setting-up exercises. Then there was an English dowager who looked as though she were held together by adhesive tape. She was betting parsimoniously, but Fletcher whispered to me that she lived in Monte Carlo on an ample allowance provided by her son-in-law, with the sole stipulation that she never embarrass the family by coming home. A moribund remittance woman. Next to her sat a pallid old gentleman whose hands, as they caressed his stack of counters, were conspicuously encased in braided gloves of gray silk. It seems that in his youth, he had been a wastrel, and, on her deathbed, his mother had squeezed from him a solemn promise never to touch card or chip again as long as he lived.

As for young White Lock, there was, until his final bet, nothing else noticeable about him except that he was the only man then at the table wearing a dinner coat. We heard later that at first he had lost heavily and had had to make several trips to the *caisse* to replenish his supply of plaques. By the time I came along he had settled to a more cautious play but finally, as if from boredom, he took all his plaques and counters and stacked them on the red. To this pile he added, just as the wheel began to turn, the contents of his wallet—emptying out a small cascade of thousand-franc notes, with a single hundred-franc note among them. But this one he retrieved at the last moment as if to be sure of carfare home. There was that breathless spinning moment, then the fateful *"Rien ne va plus,"* issuing in the same dead voice with which the intoning of the mass falls on infidel ears. Then the decision. *"Noir."* Around that table you could hear the word for black being *exhaled* in every language the world has known since Babel.

The young man gave a little laugh as the *croupier* called the turn. He sat quite still as his last gauge was raked into the bank. With all eyes on him, he shoved his chair back from the table, reached for his wallet, took out the aforesaid hundred-franc note and pushed it, with white, fastidious fingers, toward the center of the patterned baize. *"Pour le personnel,"* he said, with a kind of wry grandeur which hushed the usual twitter of thanks from the *croupiers*. "And that," he added, "is that." So saying, he got to his feet, yawned a little, and sauntered out of the room. I remember thinking, at the time, that he was behaving rather like any desperate young man in any Zoë

Akins play. But it was a good performance. And now, it seems, he lay dead by the water's edge.

It was Fletcher himself who brought the news. It came, I say, just as we were eating soufflé and talking of suicide. This, of course, was no obliging coincidence. One always tells tall tales of self-slaughter at Monte Carlo. It is part of the legend of the principality—as strong in its force of suggestion, I suppose, as the legend of Lourdes is strong in its hint to hysterics that the time has come to cast away their crutches. Fletcher told us that the sound of the shot had brought a watchman running. The youth lay on his back, his chin tilted to the stars, one outstretched hand limply holding the revolver, a dark stain on the pleated whiteness of his breast. Before Fletcher could wire his report to Paris, he would have to await certain—well—formalities. In a conspiratorial whisper, he explained there had been so many such suicides of late that a new rule was but recently put into effect. Whenever any client of the Casino was found self-slain with empty pockets, it was customary for the Casino to rush a bankroll to the spot before notifying the police, so that the victim would seem to have ended it all from *Weltschmerz*. Even now, Fletcher said, this trick must be in progress, and in the meantime he ought to be seeking such obituary data as might be gleaned in the registry office.

We were still lingering over our coffee when he came hurrying back to us, all bristling with the end of the story. Notified in due course, the *gendarmerie* had repaired to the beach in quest of the body. But there was none. Not at the indicated spot, nor anywhere else on the shore. After further search, the minor chieftain from the Casino, who had himself tucked ten thousand francs into the pocket of the now missing suicide and was still lurking, much puzzled, in the middle-distance, returned at last to the *Salles Privées,* only to find them humming with a new chapter. It seems that that young American with the white forelock—the one somebody or other had inaccurately reported as killed—had reappeared apparently restored in spirits, and certainly restored in funds. He had bet tremendously, lingered for only three turns of the wheel, and departed with a hundred thousand francs. The attendants assumed he had merely been out to dinner. At least the careless fellow had spilled some tomato sauce on his shirt front.

[1943]

# MY WICKED, WICKED WAYS

## Errol Flynn

THE COCKFIGHT IS TO THE FILIPINOS WHAT THE BULLFIGHT IS to Spain. In the Philippines they don't fool. They put a long, sharp, razor-edged, spiked spur in the heel of each cock and let them both go at it. The audience goes in for hot betting. We bought cheap tickets and watched the fighting and the betting.

When two fighting cocks are put into the arena and the bets are down, it is pretty much of an even-money go. In the case of an outstanding bird, the odds would sometimes go four to one, but that was rare.

How could we lessen the odds? How beat the Philippine game?

One day Koets flicked his fingers, slapped himself on the thigh. "Eureka!" he growled. "I have it!" That's Greek for "I've got 'em by the nuts!'" he explained.

He pulled me inside our hut and headed for his treasure chest. In one corner of the case was an old pair of socks and a small cabinet filled with colourful phials of drugs, all corked up. In another was a pile of his little black notebooks with expenses carefully enumerated on each page of each book— Dutch-efficiency style. Film equipment jammed against one of the walls of the trunk, and in another corner there was surgical equipment. "In case anyone needs a delivery or an abortion in a hurry," he said "—or fallen arches, flat feet or dandruff."

He lifted one glass phial after another. Gleefully, he held them under my nose. "See what I mean?"

I didn't.

"You dope, haven't I told you all about the snake venom that I got from the snake ranch in Rio de Janeiro?"

I still didn't follow.

"Look, have you got a small nail-file?"

I had that.

"Now listen carefully—I'll get a chicken and show you what can be done with one of these fighting cocks."

I still didn't get it, but I was getting to know the goodly doctor.

We went out, bought two chickens, returned to our little hut.

Still he wouldn't tell me what he had in mind until he started to go to work on the beaks of the two chickens.

In cockfighting in the Philippines, before the birds fight they are momentarily held about a foot apart, then the one on the right picks the comb of the one on the left. The one on the left then picks the comb of the one on the right. This makes them fighting mad, before they are allowed to tangle.

The comb, on a good fighting cock, is generally cut very low. It is a very sensitive part of the bird. It is soft and, if pecked, it may open easily.

"Now watch," said Koets. He serrated the edge of the beak of one of the cocks with the nail-file, making it sharp as a pin point. He put three little grooves in the beak, turning it into a vital fang. He put a dab of snake venom on the beak.

We were ready for the experiment.

I held in my hand the bird whose beak hadn't been tampered with. Koets held the cock with the poisoned beak. I let my bird take a peck out of the comb of the one Koets held. Then he let his bird take a bite out of the comb of mine.

We timed them. How long would it take for the poison in the beak of Koets's bird to affect my chicken?

We put them down and they circled a minute, then flew at each other. In a very few seconds the bird without the poison in his beak toppled over and lay dying. The venom had taken effect.

We ran out and bought four birds. Just ordinary birds which cost us almost nothing. We'd turn them into champs in a jiffy.

Armed with four superb fighters, we headed for the cock-fights. We entered our birds and 'handicapped' hard.

The odds were always against our birds. They were such scrubby-looking things, but miraculously we won, for Koets had plenty of phials of that Brazilian snake venom in his magic treasure chest.

Koets believed that snake venom had many qualities not yet known to science, curative and destructive. He had hoped to experiment with it—but now he had found the greatest use of all. Snakes never paid off so well before in the history of venomous ideas.

Every now and then we would drop a fight, just for the sake of appearances, but, generally speaking, our business was safer than that of the Bank of England.

We moved into another house. We bought new suits. We dressed smartly. That was always important to me at that time. I looked like a dude, sported a cane, and carried a fighting cock under my arm, like a pet poodle.

The place we lived in overlooked Manila Bay. The girls came, the girls went.

Cockfights started at seven o'clock promptly each evening, and sometimes there was a second round of fights at ten o'clock.

It was my job to lay the bets since I spoke better Spanish than Koets. It was his, as the scientist, to keep the birds in fine form, their beaks sharp. We even invested heavily in several brand-new nail-files, the only tool we needed.

Bets were paying off so regularly and we were doing so well that Koets was running short of snake juice.

We were doing so well we should have known it couldn't last.

One night I ran around in my usual fashion soliciting bets. *"Si, cuanto, cuanto? Bueno bueno, viejo."* I passed a slip of paper up to somebody prepared to bet. He passed me down his money. I did the bookmaking. I carried a long black bag slung over my shoulders, and in this I held the fine Manila pesos.

This night I was running around, smiling, saying *"viejo"*, meaning "old boy", to my clients, and placing bets. They suspected nothing. They just thought they had bad luck and we had good luck.

Everything was set. The bets were high.

We were now entering a cock who had won three straight fights in a row. He was practically a contender for the championship of Manila.

I was taking the bets when I felt a hot, heavy breath on my neck. It was Koets's. "How much have you got?" he asked.

"Plenty."

"Fine. I've booked a side bet. If it doesn't conflict with your bookings we stand to win ten thousand pesos." At the time that would be about three or four thousand dollars.

The tiers went up, colosseum-fashion, in this arena. A crowd of thousands looked down from their gallery seats.

In their corner the seconds were handling their champ bird, called The Flower. All fighting cocks have names. Ours was named Strike by Night. The Flower had been well trained for weeks and looked beautiful. He was striped and he was making fighting noises. Our bird was smaller, but looked vicious enough. To look at these two fowl, anyone would pick the other to win.

Because our bird was smaller we got large odds—four to one. It is even possible that a few Filipinos may have suspected by now our endless run of luck. Two strangers, and they seemed to know more about cockfighting than the natives.

The fight was ready to start. Everybody was standing in the tiers.

As yet Koets had not placed the venom on the bird's beak.

This he learned to do very subtly, like a magician, taking a small bit of cotton wool, which he could hide between his fingers, and placing it on the bird's beak the instant before the ritual of letting the birds peck each other.

Koets cleverly took care of the last detail. The speck of cotton wool slipped into his pocket unnoticed.

The birds were brought together for the bite of challenge before the fight. The handlers held them face to face. Each picked the comb of the other.

They were dropped on to the ground as the handlers went back to their corners.

The whole house was silent as the two birds circled.

Two cocks that had been brought together like that would fly at each other the instant they were put on the ground, or while they were in the air, but these two were wary. They circled far longer than two cocks ordinarily would.

They wheeled, each looking for an opening.

Round and round they went, making of this fight a carousel of slow timing.

All of a sudden the other bird, The Flower, without a blow having been struck, wheeled over dead. There he was, spurs up, in his death throes.

Our Strike by Night went in for a needless kill, jumping on The Flower and pecking at him with no mercy, little knowing that The Flower was already as stiff as the last chicken in the cold freeze.

My back was to the birds. I was still taking bets. I thought something odd was going on when I heard a shout of surprise from the whole gallery. I turned and took a look. The sound got louder. A tremendous eruption from the fans. The officials were excited.

At just that instant Koets's hand sank into my shoulder as if he wanted to take a hunk of meat out of it. *"Alt, alt, rares,"* he called. He looked distraught.

"What's the matter?"

"Don't ask now! Let's get the hell out of here while we're still ahead!"

He held me in that policeman's grip.

"For Christ's sake, let's get going!"

"Where?"

"Anywhere!"

We managed to get out. As we scurried through the streets we had no way of knowing what was happening back at the arena.

We padded as fast as we could back to our lodging. "All we can take is the cameras and the money," Koets said. "Grab the cameras and let's get to the wharf."

We had in our pockets, in Philippine pesos, about the equivalent of $4,000.

We snatched the treasure chest, left all our clothes. We got a horse and buggy cab that took us, via side streets, to the pier.

We didn't know what boat we'd get on, or whether we would get one, or whether there'd be one. We only knew that boats left every hour. East, south, west, north—no matter—just get on something that floated and leave—even if it went back to New Guinea.

We arrived at the pier. Sure enough, a steamer was going out. It was the *Empress of Asia*, a big ancient-looking tub. We rushed up the gangplank, without tickets, only our passports.

For a while we hid in a stateroom. As the boat made ready to leave, we ventured out on deck to take a look at the shore. When the gangplank was being drawn up we saw, on the wharf, an excited crowd of Filipinos. Some pointing at the ship, some at the arena. They were gesticulating, arguing, yelling at the police.

There was no point in nostalgic farewells. We scrammed back to our rooms, hoping the boat would pull out.

When we felt the motion of the ship we began breathing easier again.

I asked, "Where do you suppose this boat is going?"

"Let's go find out," suggested Koets.

On deck I made inquiries. First stop, Hong Kong.

I gave Koets a jubilant jab in the ribs. "Look at 'em. Still brandishing bolos."

Koets grinned.

"About as close as we'll ever come," I said.

"I didn't know I could run that fast," Koets mused.

He looked around the ship. "Good God!" he cried, striking his head.

"What's up?" I had a sudden horrible thought we had been trailed aboard ship by the Filipino police.

"Do you know where we are?"

I told him yes, on the *Empress of Asia.*

"Yes, but in *first*-class!"

The idea of travelling first-class was anathema to him. The cost! The mere idea appalled him. He had certain scruples about the wealthy, the mighty, the utilities. Don't pay them a cent more than you have to. Don't enrich the rich. Outwit them, yes; that was reasonable.

"But look," I objected, "we're loaded with dough. We can travel any way we want. In style, old boy."

"And give those thieves the difference? They're a bunch of crooks!" His big broad face flushed. "Not that I mind parting with the money"—he did mind, very much—"but I take pride in doing the world at minimum cost. By God, I'm off. Are you coming?"

No, I wasn't. It was only a short trip to Hong Kong. I was going first-class—a matter of principle.

"Be seeing you," said Koets, stomping off.

He could find his way about a ship better than a ship's cat. He spent practically all of his time in first-class, although paying steerage fare. If you could do it that way, I decided, it made some sense.

[1959]

# FAKING ORGASMS

## Shere Hite

THE PRESSURE ON WOMEN TO ORGASM DURING INTERCOURSE is so great that an enormous number of women fake orgasms— some infrequently, most "sometimes," but some women said they do it every single time.

| *DO YOU FAKE ORGASMS?* | |
|---|---:|
| *Yes* | *567* |
| *No* | *775* |
| *Used to* | *318* |
| *"It's no use, it's not convincing"* | *4* |
| *Total* | *1,664* |

"I used to fake orgasms all the time, and always with vaginal penetration. I came from the school of it's not right—you'll emasculate the man—if you don't let him think he's satisfied you. With the onset of the women's movement, and its personal effect on me, I've stopped faking them. My husband used to ask, 'Did you come?'—and when the answer was 'yes'—even if I was faking it—that was cool for him. Then when I started saying 'no' a couple of times, he quit asking. Now, if I complain I didn't come, he's either asleep, or says he's sorry and turns over and goes to sleep."

"I never fake orgasm. I am angry with other women who do, because then men can tell me that I am incapable sexually, because I do not have vaginal climaxes, and other women they have slept with do. Since I have never had a vaginal climax, I question their existence, or at least their general prevalence, and wonder if another woman's faking an orgasm has made it harder for me when I am honest."

"I fake it during clitoral stimulation and during intercourse when I'm not in the mood. It's easier and faster than saying 'no' and then worrying about my husband's ego and feelings for me, etc. He, like most other men, gets really frightened and hurt when I say 'no' and I hear about it in passing a week later."

"I have, and occasionally still do fake orgasms during intercourse, but not often. When I do it now it's because I know I'm not going to have an orgasm but my man is working really hard for me and really wants to give me one and would be very disappointed to know it's no use. As we live together longer it becomes less necessary because our sex is better and we know each other better. In the past I would do it to protect the man's ego and occasionally (with one man) because he would be mad if I didn't have one. I hate faking it, though, and I really hated it with that one man, but he was a typical dominant egocentric chauvinistic horse's ass."

"During my marriage I was excellent at faking orgasms and so for maybe four years I never really had any satisfying sexual experiences. Unfortunately, I was totally faithful to my husband so I was pretty miserable physically. I masturbated a whole lot! After my separation I explored sex with a variety of partners and had a sexual awakening, so to speak."

"Yes, I used to, more to give a positive reinforcement for something I liked even though I didn't orgasm."

"I used to, when my husband had a complex about sex and a marriage counselor told me I should build up his ego."

"No, but I may act more excited than I really am."

"I used to, because my partner was comparing me to another woman he was sleeping with. He made me feel terrible with descriptions of how she went into a screaming orgasm before he even entered her."

"Yes, when I haven't had one for quite a while, I do it so my partner won't think he isn't pleasing me. I don't feel orgasms are all that important (he seems to) and I don't feel it's his fault if I don't come but . . . sometimes it is his fault, though, I guess."

"I was afraid to appear 'less of a woman' and demasculate my partner. So I did it, but he found me out."

"Sometimes it builds a man's ego to let him think he's successful. Therefore if I really like a man and want him to think I enjoyed sex more than I did, I do it."

"Only to get me or him 'off the hook.'"

"For fifteen years I was the world's best faker. Honestly— they should have a phallic trophy—mounted on a pedestal (like in the art history books) for *all women*—I think they all fake it with men."

[1976]

# THE SECRET LIFE OF
# HAROLD WINNEY

## James Thurber


HAROLD WINNEY, WHO SEEMED TO ME, AND STILL DOES, unreal as the look and sound of his name, was Ross's private secretary from 1935 until the middle of August, 1941. In his years with Ross, the pallid, silent young man steadily swindled the editor out of a total of seventy-one thousand dollars. His multiple forgeries, his raids and inroads upon Ross's bank account, expense account, salary, and securities, belong in McKelway's *Of Crime and Rascality*, somewhere between the magnificently complicated defalcations of the Wily Wilby and the fantastic dollar bill counterfeiting of Old 880. Bankers, tax men, and accountants still shake their heads in wonder and disbelief over the case history of Harold Winney, which has become a part of the folklore and curiosa of American capitalism.

Nobody at the *New Yorker* offices knew, or cared, very much about Harold Winney, who had been born about 1910 in or near Albany, New York, the only child of a man who died when his son was very young, and of a mother who fortunately did not live long enough to know about her son's crimes. I remember Winney mainly for his cold small voice, his pale nimble fingers, and his way of moving about the corridors and offices like a shadow. I do not believe that Harold Ross ever looked at the man closely enough to have been able to describe him accurately. He was what Ross once irritably described as a "worm"—that is, an unimportant cog in the *New Yorker* wheel, a noncreative person. As a secretary, Winney was competent and quiet.

He took dictation speedily, and transcribed his notes the same way. I would be sitting in my office, and suddenly his voice would surprise me, for I never heard him enter the room. "Mr. Ross would like your opinion on this," he would say, and hand me a typewritten query about something or other; this was in the days when I could see to read. He would stand there absolutely motionless, without a word, and wait for me to tell him what I thought, or to type my reply on a piece of paper; then he would silently vanish. He was master of the art of protective immobility. I remember that he was neat to the point of being immaculate, but the clothes he wore were as unobtrusive as his manner. When investigators examined his apartment, they found, among other things, a hundred and three suits of clothes which he had bought with the money stolen from Ross. They also found, in a private correspondence file, a long exchange of letters with a real estate firm in Tahiti. Winney had planned, a little vaguely, to flee when he had piled up enough of his employer's money, but the embezzler never does get enough, and when, in the the summer of 1941, his crimes were discovered, the war was on and he could not obtain a passport.

Discovery, in the end, was inevitable. The miracle is that it didn't come years sooner. If Winney drank or smoked, it was usually in moderation, and there was only one subject in the world that could light up his cold eyes and his impassive face. That was horse racing. He was a horse player, completely addicted to it, and a steady loser. Nobody will ever know how much he lost in gambling on the horses, or what exactly became of the seventy-one thousand dollars he stole. Copies of his private letters to men friends revealed that he spent his money lavishly upon some of them, buying one an expensive sports car, outfitting another with complete skiing equipment, and giving them money for their vacations and holidays. Investigators were baffled at every turn in trying to trace what happened to Ross's money. There was, however, a record of a big champagne party Winney gave in a suite at the Astor Hotel on the night in November, 1940, when Roosevelt was elected President for the third time. "I walked past the Astor several times that night with friends," Ross told me gloomily, "and I guess I was hit on the head by my own champagne corks." He gestured toward the room just outside his own office where Winney had had his desk and typewriter. "He sat out there and fed me cake," Ross moaned.

Winney was, by a familiar caprice of nature, incapable of emotional interest in females, and this was as apparent to all of us, except Ross, as the simple fact that Mary Pickford is a woman. To Ross, however, who never scrutinized his secretary or gave him any real thought, he was nothing more than a chair in his office or the ash tray on his desk. "Did you know he was *that* kind of a man?" Ross asked me and the rest of us, and we all just stared at him and said, "Yes, didn't you?" Ross would brush this aside and say, "Then it explains the whole business. That kind of guy always wants to ruin the normal man."

Ross was by no means, of course, financially ruined by Winney, for he still had plenty of money of his own after the loss of the seventy-one thousand dollars.

During the almost seven years that Winney robbed Ross, day after day, the editor was at the peak of his work and his worries in every field. In 1935, the year Winney came to work for him, Ross's daughter was born, and the magazine was developing rapidly in every way. In the midst of all this, Ross recognized the necessity of "delegating" some of his duties and some of his worries. He made the big mistake of delegating to Harold Winney complete control, without any safeguard whatever, of his bank accounts and securities—he had two separate accounts in one bank. The bank tellers and vice-presidents became familiar with the quiet, well-behaved, efficient young man who was Ross's private secretary, and in whom, the editor had made it clear, he reposed every trust. Thus, when Winney showed up at the teller's cage with a check made out to cash, signed with the unmistakable signature of H. W. Ross, the check was not subjected to more than casual scrutiny. Even if it had been, Winney's forgery of Ross's name was so perfect that after the secretary's death, the few canceled checks that could be found baffled not only handwriting experts but even Ross himself, who could not swear whether a given signature was his own or Winney's. Winney's own initials were H. W. and all he had to imitate were the six letters of H. W. Ross. He became an expert at it.

As the years went on, he grew bolder and bolder, and in one week, the record shows, cashed three separate checks for a total of six thousand dollars. At that period, Ross's main financial interest was in his friend Dave Chasen's restaurant in Hollywood. About the time that Harold Winney began robbing Ross, the restaurant began to make money. Ross had originally lent Chasen three thousand dollars, a generous personal loan of the kind for which he was well known to his intimates. Sums of money like that did not bother Ross when it came to helping out one of the men to whom he was most devoted. Later he began investing in the restaurant and his profits increased, but he could never quite accommodate himself to the idea that he deserved the profits, which amounted finally to more than two hundred thousand dollars. "Goddam it, I never intended to make a lot of money of out Dave's place," he once told a lawyer. "It's hard for me to think he owes me anything, except on the basis of personal loans." The difference between a loan and an investment had to be explained to him patiently. "I know, I know all that," he would say, putting on his well-known expression of worry and wonder.

Winney began cautiously by forging six checks in 1935 for a total of about fourteen hundred dollars; the next year he forged seven checks for a total of nineteen hundred dollars. In 1937 there were nine checks, and the amount was twenty-nine hundred dollars, and in 1938, the year before he threw caution to the winds, he forged seven checks for twenty-seven hundred and thirty dollars. During all this time he was careful to fill out checkbook stubs and reconcile them precisely with Ross's monthly bank statements. He had soon discovered, but probably couldn't believe it, that Ross did not want to be bothered by studying his checkbooks or monthly statements. So Winney "summarized" them, as he explained it to Ross, and would simply lay a typed sheet of paper on Ross's desk when he was asked about the state of his account. If Ross spotted some familiar amount, such as $113.13, and said, "I thought that check went through last month," Winney would simply tell him quietly that he was wrong. The cake became easier and easier to feed to Ross, and Winney finally abandoned entirely the unnecessary work of justification. He would simply tear a check out of a checkbook, fill it out for whatever amount he wanted, sign Ross's name, and cash it at the bank. When he really began to splurge with Ross's money and visit the bank several times a week, he would hand in the check and wink slyly at the teller, as if to say, "The old boy's at it again." I don't know how many persons, outside the *New Yorker* and Ross's circle of friends, knew how often Ross gambled and how often he lost, but it was scarcely a state secret. Dozen of checks for gambling losses, averaging around five hundred dollars, were duplicated by Winney before he sent them, with Ross's genuine signature on them, to the lucky winners. During 1939 and 1940 and up until the end of July, 1941, Winney forged a hundred and sixty checks for a total of about sixty-two thousand dollars. By the end of July, 1941, he had withdrawn all of his employer's salary through December and, along with it, several thousand dollars of Ross's expense account money.

Winney was a well-implemented student of his employer. He was, however, at all times skating on ice that grew thinner and thinner, and he must have known that sooner or later it would break under him. It may be that he hoped to restore the money he had taken if he could only win a large amount on the horses or make some quick and profitable investment, but nobody knows about that, or if anybody does, nothing has ever been revealed. Winney's friends, or such of them as were found and talked to, claimed they knew nothing about his secret life, and this may well have been true. He was as tight-mouthed as he was thin-lipped.

The withdrawal in advance of Ross's salary and expense account money had to be accomplished through the *New Yorker's* own business department, and, in spite of the tension between the editor and that department, it remained something of a miracle that nothing was said to Ross about these massive withdrawals until the middle of August, 1941. One man in the business department, who has been there for more than thirty years, told me what I already knew: that if the business department ever mentioned money to Ross, he yelled them down, or said they were crazy, or announced that he didn't want to talk about it and hung up the phone. There were years during which he would refuse to discuss anything at all with Fleischmann, and such communications as passed between them were carried on circuitously. Winney was also a close student of this situation.

In 1938 Ross and his second wife spent several months in France and England, and before he left he put his securities in Winney's hands, giving him power of attorney over them. In order to replenish this or that account, in a crisis, the secretary would sell some of Ross's securities. Ross both played into Winney's hands and made things a bit difficult for him by carrying loose checks in his pocket and making them out to this person or that or to this firm or that, sometimes remembering to tell Winney about them the next day, but often forgetting it. In this way, Winney could never be sure what situation would confront him at the end of any given month.

During the last year of Winney's peculations, he caused Ross to be overdrawn multiple times at the bank. When this situation occurred, Winney would either transfer some funds from the account in Jane Grant's name to Ross's own account, or cover up by selling some more of Ross's securities. The "mad, intelligent Ross," as Janet Flanner once called him, had simply forgotten to cancel Winney's power of attorney, after the editor got back from France. Ross expected to get loyalty from those around him the way he expected to get his mail, but he didn't always get that, either. All communications from the bank and several letters from a firm of tax experts, suggesting that they supervise Ross's financial interests, were simply torn up and thrown away by Ross's secretary.

When it comes to money, bank accounts, and everything else fiscal or financial, I am not one to throw stones, but a pot as black as the kettle. I once had a checking account in a famous old Fifth Avenue bank, through the recommendation of Ralph Ingersoll, but after I had been overdrawn three times, I was invited to talk it over with a vice-president of the bank. He was shocked almost beyond words when he discovered that I did not fill out my checkbook stubs. "Then how do you know how much money you have in the bank?" he asked me, and I told him, "I estimate it." He turned a little white and his hand trembled. "You—*estimate* it?" he croaked. That bank was glad to get rid of me.

I have always had the good sense to let my wife handle my finances, but Ross would just have goggled at anyone who suggested that he put such a responsibility upon his own spouse. It was not only his strangeness about dough, but his erratic judgments of men, that put such a powerful temptation in the way of Harold Winney. One of those around him in the early years, a man he both liked and trusted, and rightly so, was Ralph Paladino. When he was young and single, Ralph took a course in public accounting at a night school, and Ross attended his graduation exercises. Ralph, it seemed to us in those days, kept track of everything for Ross. He was an expert on order, organization, dough, records, and everything else that Ross worried about. Then Ralph was married and after a while had children, and needed an increase of salary, and Ross would not okay this. I still get mad at him when I think about it, and I once bawled him out for it, after Ralph quit and took a better-paying job. "I haven't got time for little people," Ross snarled, and I told him that was a hell of a thing to say. He later apologized for it, murmered something about all the physical troubles that he had at the time, a jaw infection, his ulcers, and the spreading of the metatarsal bones of one foot. Ralph Paladino, by the way, is now head of the make-up department at *Newsweek*. Last year a man who works there told me, "He is our one most indispensable man."

Harold Ross had a lot of thing to think about in 1941, including his approaching third marriage, three of my five eye operations, the war and all that it did to him, and a hundred other concerns. He himself had withdrawn some of his salary and expense account that year, and this gave Winney the idea of withdrawing the rest of it. Such transactions as this had to be okayed by the Miracle Man—during most of this period it was Ik Shuman. One day after Winney had withdrawn Ross's salary and expense money for October, November, and December, Raoul Fleischmann sent for Shuman and said, "Did you know that Ross is hard up?" They discussed the matter, and Ik said he would look into it.

For a while Ross simply did not believe, or even listen to, what Shuman had to tell him about his withdrawn salary. Then he sent for Winney. That doomed young man knew that he had come to the end of the line, but he didn't turn white, or begin shaking, or break down and confess. He simply double-talked Ross into deeper and deeper confusion, until the editor said, "Oh, the hell with it—I'll stop in at the bank tomorrow and find out all about it myself." That sentence was Harold Winney's death sentence. After work he went home to his expensive and tidily furnished apartment in Brooklyn, turned on the gas in the kitchen and took his own life.

When the body of Harold Winney was discovered the next day in his Brooklyn apartment, Ross was greatly upset, and when the first batch of his manifold forgeries came to light, he expressed pity for him, and even compassion, according to Shuman and Gene Kinkead, Ross's great "gumshoe." Kinkead had been assigned to find out as much as he could about what Winney had done to Ross, and when the staggering total of the quiet man's thefts became clear, Ross no longer said, as he had been saying, "The poor little guy." What mainly bothered Ross, however, was not the amount of his losses, but the feeling that his "friends at 21," as Shuman put it, would never get over kidding him about it all. So the actual total of the forgeries was not given out to the papers. They were told that it was somewhere between seventeen thousand and twenty thousand dollars. That's what Ross told me, too. I think that he was wrong about this. Any American can be taken for seventeen thousand or twenty thousand dollars, but it takes a really great eccentric to be robbed of seventy-one thousand dollars right under his busy nose.

I am told that Ross could not be reimbursed by the bank for his losses, because he had made this legally impossible by the way he ignored his monthly statements, and by his giving power of attorney to Winney, which he never withdrew. It seems that Ross did get five thousand dollars of Harold Winney's insurance money. What I remember mainly about the wreckage of that tragic August was a strange threat Ross made. He was going to get even with the bank, he said, by "hiring Steve Hannagan." Just what he expected that late, famous public relations man, sometimes known as the "Discoverer of Florida," to do, I have no way of knowing. Ross soon realized, of course, that publicity was precisely what he did not want.

Among those to whom Ross occasionally lost money at backgammon or gin rummy was a well-known New York publisher, and whenever he won from two hundred dollars to five hundred dollars from Ross, Winney would duplicate the check, so that Ross really always lost twice as much as he believed he had. Losing anything to a publisher was, to H. W. Ross, something that there could be nothing more deplorable than. He fought publishers, on behalf of writers, all his life, and wrote literally hundreds of letters bawling them out. One of these, to Marshall Best, runs to two thousand words. In a letter to Ross, the publisher had accused him of obscurantism, and Ross ended his reply, "Whee! Let's have oceans of obscurantism." Ross and the *New Yorker* never took any subsidiary rights at all from writers and artists, but were satisfied with first serial rights. When Ross found out that publishers often got a percentage of their authors' sales of movie or theater rights, he banged away at them on his trusty typewriter, and you could hear it all the way down the hall. He also fought them for better royalties for writers and for a more equable arrangement on anthologies. He once got a letter from Christopher La Farge, then president of the Authors' League, thanking him, on behalf of the authors of the country, for what he had been doing and was still doing.

I don't know how to end this account of the short, unhappy life of Harold Winney, but I guess I'll just put down what two different admirers of Ross, who did not know the Winney story, said, in the same voice, after I had told the tale. "What a wonderful man!" said one of them. "What a crazy guy!" said the other.

[1959]

# IT'S ON THE HOUSE!

## Stanley Bing

A FRIEND WHO WORKS IN KUALA LUMPUR FOR THE Weaselfreund Corporation of Ypsilanti, Michigan, writes: "Next month I'm having a large dinner party for *tout le monde* in the Bagged Waste Treatment subculture here in town. All my peers will be there: Barry Switzlinger of Global Crude, Edie St. Bacobitz from Eastermaus, their subordinates, their subordinates' subordinates, most of my staff. Possibly even several representatives of the former Republican administration who are now serving on the boards of friendly corporations around the nation will be there, as long as we're willing to send transport for them, even those who are within walking distance. Total number of people who are expected to be in attendance: one hundred. Dinner is traditional: turkey, oyster stuffing, haricots verts, and six kinds of sparkling water, followed by at least a liter of champagne per guest. Afterward each guest will expect to be conveyed back to his or her residence by personal rickshaw. Since this event will be manifestly of a business nature, and since under no circumstance would I subject myself, my residence, or my family to such indignity otherwise, and since the fete will most likely cost in the vicinity of several thousand dinars, may I attempt to pass through this exorbitant business cost on my monthly expense voucher? The whole event is semimandatory; such lenten entertainments are expected of me as evidence of my probity and standing in the business community. Why should I hoof the bill when my company could eat it without a belch? Well? should I . . . dare I . . . expense it?"

I don't know, pal. Can you get away with it?

In these lean and Spartan days, when salary increases hover in the low single digits and all official perks are viewed through a rheumy eye, the entire issue of business expense rears up before us, growling, snapping, and displaying a nasty set of unflossed teeth. Which side are you on? Are you one of those cocktail wieners who are content to tread the same old tired path of received wisdom—and pay for things yourself like a nineteenth-century honest person? Or do you stand with the new generation of thinkers who are attempting to redefine the entire notion of business expense, moving ever closer to the incandescent, orgasmic moment when, yes, yes, one's entire existence is placed on official life-support? Could such a thing be possible?

I assure you: It is. You can get there, too, if you work with me here.

First, we'll need to evaluate which stratum of the corporate-expense food chain you inhabit and what you can do about it.

**LEVEL ONE:** *Itsy-bitsy Nerdling.*
A friend in the cheese-repackaging group of a major multinational conglomerate headquartered in Hortense, Missouri, writes: "I want to have a sandwich, but I don't want to pay for it. Can I get the company to pay for it?"

Straighten up, man! You're a pathetic wart on the backside of civilization. Every soda, newspaper, and taxicab that you dare to take is dealt with on an individual basis. Every time you go to a restaurant with your buddies (who, after all, are in the same business as you—and possibly even more influential!), you are forced to either fork over actual cash for your share of the festivities or, infinitely worse, hitch a ride on their corporate plastic, mumbling something like "getcha next time" under your breath. You want to be on the planet! You want people to murmur, "Gee, I had no idea he was a hitter of such extraordinary dimensions!" In short, you want your importance to be overestimated, just like everybody else. Just do it, Spud. You'll never get out and up otherwise. Starting right now, once every ten days or so, incur some moderate expense (in the neighborhood of thirty-five dollars) that is absolutely, undeniably of good business import. Meals out of town on heroic business missions are perfect. Drinks with a critical industry reporter are also good. Take a consultant for a slab of pale fish if you must. But establish a weekly expense that seems to be justified, reasonable, and, most important, regular.

Do that until you're all growed up. Then come back ready to party.

**LEVEL TWO:** *Dress for Excess.*
A friend from the chip-and-dip-switch division of a computer-entrail manufacturer writes: "After years of trying, I now have a respectable expense account, but it's closely supervised and almost impossible to abuse. What should I do?"

Step up to the plate, Bud. Your policy is now to push the envelope until it is the size of a goiter that travels wherever you do and is just about as obvious. Up there in the stratosphere, there are guys whose HBO subscriptions are comped because they need to stay informed about the state of movie-deal back ends. Guys who get a clothing allotment, for Chrissakes. Keep your mind on all those injustices as you go about generating your own.

Secrecy is out. You want people to know right out in the open that you're producing value for the company—and that costs money. In a major city, that means establishing a consis-tent level of abuse, say, $1,000 per month, just to pick a num-ber out of a hat. That breaks down to $50 per day—about enough for a respectable power lunch in a second-rate town or a magnificent daily breakfast just about anyplace. Keep all expenditures well under the level where a capital review would be implemented, but never let them drop too low or people will start questioning your whole conceptual package. Don't, on the other hand, be a greedy nitwit with juice dripping down his chin. One guy I know charged all the furniture in his house to the company, for example. He got fired, naturally, for two reasons. First, he wasn't a big enough dude to be that venal. Second, he tried to hide it. People hate a liar who gets caught.

In your ongoing campaign, remember: Keep it steady. Build up week by week, month by month. Don't attract attention to yourself. There was this corporate politician who worked at my company before I got here, Kenny Leming. Although it's never been adjudicated, speculation has it the guy was a cocaine addict. He sure spent money like one. Every day he would take an advance against expenses of $200. That's okay. But for more than a year he just plain didn't file an expense report. When he did, the amount he had advanced himself was in the neighborhood of $30,000. He had to exceed that amount on his eventual statement in order to come away with a little walking-around money. That, not his taste for nasal freezer burn or ridiculous limos, is what is remembered about him. "Yeah, Kenny Leming," people will say, and shake their heads. "Wasn't that the guy that presented Carl with a $40,000 expense statement?"

Keep in mind, by the way, that five statements of $8,000 each would probably have been fine and might even have been interpreted, after all the facts were in, as management of a ticklish problem. Financial manipulation isn't against the rules, you know. Actually, it *is* the rules.

**LEVEL THREE:** *The Triumph of the Will.*
A friend from the Japanese subsidiary of a U. S. convenience-store chain writes: "My corporation needed to pay off some gangsters who were threatening to release bad information about us. The money came from my personal bank account. Although I am filled with shame over the entire incident, I

still would like to know whether I should put through an expense report on this sum."

Absolutely! You're in the big time now. The entity you're orbiting is one of the most beautiful in all the business universe. It's a black hole, a place so heavy with executive weight that no personal responsibility can escape. Relax as your entire lifestyle is sucked into its center and down, down into the depths of the company's capacious bourse. You are It. It is You. Have a nice day. You're a key chunk of stellar material in the established firmament, so all objects worn, all food eaten, all trips taken (and frequent-flyer miles, too!), all gifts and costly special occasions, all vehicles and habits, are paid for without question by the business. Golf is free. Skiing sometimes, too. All of it. How do you get there? I'll tell you how you get there! You get a car, that's how you get there! The car comes first, the rest comes next. Until you have the car, you've got squat.

A man without free wheels has yet to cross that mythical bridge into the utter existential annihilation of self, the total oneness with the massive feed bag that characterizes the executive lifestyle. Me, I'm getting a Lincoln Town Car. They're huge. So will I be, when I'm in one. With the car comes mileage. And gas, too. Then I want to drive my big fat car to my big fat house, which has to be enormous because a man of my standing needs to put a huge face on stuff so, as a business tool, it's expensed too, you know, and my kids have to go to school with the children of my peers and my competitors, and that costs what, maybe twenty grand a year—that would not be necessary if I were not such a tremendous dude, so I'm going to put that through also, and my wife! She's expensive too! And I don't want to pay for her either! Let the company do it! Because I'm large! I'm gargantuan! And my life is utterly, totally, completely liberated from the human reality under which lesser mortals function—and it's free! Free! Free! And I love it! For as long as it lasts, I adore it! Yum! Smack! *Goooood!*

And finally . . . what's this?

A friend who works for the . . . Internal Revenue Service . . . writes in to ask: "Have you declared all this stuff you're getting as income?"

[1993]

# MY MOTHER'S MEMOIRS, MY FATHER'S LIE, AND OTHER TRUE STORIES

## Russell Banks

MY MOTHER TELLS ME STORIES ABOUT HER PAST, AND I DON'T believe them, I interpret them.

She told me she had the female lead in the Catamount High School senior play and Sonny Tufts had the male lead. She claimed that he asked her to the cast party, but by then she was in love with my father, a stagehand for the play, so she turned down the boy who became a famous movie actor and went to the cast party with the boy who became a New Hampshire carpenter.

She also told me that she knew the principals in Grace Metalious's novel *Peyton Place*. The same night the girl in the book murdered her father, she went afterwards to a Christmas party given by my mother and father in Catamount. "The girl acted strange," my mother said. "Kind of like she was on drugs or something, you know? And the boy she was with, one of the Goldens. He just got drunk and depressed, and then they left. The next day we heard about the police finding the girl's father in the manure pile . . . ."

"Manure pile?"

"She buried him there. And your father told me to keep quiet, not to tell a soul they were at our party on Christmas Eve. That's why our party isn't in the book or the movie they made of it," she explained.

She also insists, in the face of my repeated denials, that she once saw me being interviewed on television by Dan Rather.

I remembered these three stories recently when, while pawing through a pile of old newspaper clippings, I came upon the obituary of Sonny Tufts. Since my adolescence, I have read two and sometimes three newspapers a day, and frequently I clip an article that for obscure or soon forgotten reasons attracts me; then I toss the clipping into a desk drawer, and every once in a while, without scheduling it, I am moved to read through the clippings and throw them out. It's an experience that fills me with a strange sadness, a kind of grief for my lost self, as if I were reading and throwing out old diaries.

But it's my mother I was speaking of. She grew up poor and beautiful in a New England mill town, Catamount, New Hampshire, the youngest of the five children of a machinist whose wife died ("choked to death on a porkchop bone"— another of her stories) when my mother was nineteen. She was invited the same year, 1933, to the Chicago World's Fair to compete in a beauty pageant but didn't accept the invitation, though she claims my father went to the fair and played his clarinet in a National Guard marching band. Her father, she said, made her stay in Catamount that summer, selling dresses for Grover Cronin's Department Store on River Street. If her mother had not died that year, she would have been able to go to the fair. "And who knows," she joked, "you might've ended up the son of Miss Chicago World's Fair of 1933."

To tell the truth, I don't know very much about my mother's life before 1940, the year I was born and started gathering material for my own stories. Like most people, I pay scant attention to the stories I'm told about lives and events that precede the remarkable event of my own birth. We all seem to tell and hear our own memoirs. It's the same with my children. I watch their adolescent eyes glaze over, their attention drift on to secret plans for the evening and weekend, as I point out the tenement on Perley Street in Catamount where I spent my childhood. Soon it will be too late, I want to say. Soon I, too, will be living in exile, retired from the cold like my mother in San Diego, alone in a drab apartment in a project by the bay, collecting social security and wondering if I'll have enough money at the end of the month for a haircut. Soon all you'll have of me will be your memories of my stories.

Everyone knows that the death of a parent is a terrible thing. But because our parents usually have not been a part of our daily lives for years, most of us do not miss them when they die. When my father died, even though I had been seeing him frequently and talking with him on the phone almost every week, I did not miss him. Yet his death was for me a terrible thing and goes on being a terrible thing now, five years later. My father, a depressed, cynical alcoholic, did not tell stories, but even if he had told stories—about his childhood in Nova Scotia, about beating out Sonny Tufts in the courtship of my mother, about playing the clarinet at the Chicago World's Fair—I would not have listened. No doubt, in his cynicism and despair of ever being loved, he knew that.

The only story my father told me that I listened to closely, visualized, and have remembered, he told me a few months before he died. It was the story of how he came to name me Earl. Naturally, as a child I asked, and he simply shrugged and said he happened to like the name. My mother corroborated the shrug. But one Sunday morning the winter before he died, three years before he planned to retire and move to a trailer down south, I was sitting across from my father in his kitchen, watching him drink tumblers of Canadian Club and ginger ale, and he wagged a finger in my face and told me that I did not know who I was named after.

"I thought no one," I said.

"When I was a kid," he said, "my parents tried to get rid of me in the summers. They used to send me to stay with my Uncle Earl up on Cape Breton. He was a bachelor and kind of a hermit, and he stayed drunk most of the time. But he played the fiddle, the violin. And he loved me. He was quite a character. But then, when I was about twelve, I was old enough to spend my summers working, so they kept me down in Halifax after that. And I never saw Uncle Earl again."

He paused and sipped at his drink. He was wearing his striped pajamas and maroon bathrobe and carpet slippers and was chain-smoking Parliaments. His wife (his second—my mother divorced him when I was twelve, because of his drinking and what went with it) had gone to the market as soon as I arrived, as if afraid to leave him without someone else in the house. "He died a few years later," my father said. "Fell into a snowbank, I heard. Passed out. Froze to death."

I listened to the story and have remembered it today because I thought it was about *me*, my name, Earl. My father told it, of course, because it was about *him*, and because for an instant that cold February morning he dared to hope that his oldest son would love him.

At this moment, as I say this, I do love him, but it's too late for the saying to make either of us happy. That is why I say the death of a parent is a terrible thing.

After my father died, I asked his sister Ethel about poor old Uncle Earl. She said she never heard of the man. The unofficial family archivist and only a few years younger than my father, she surely would have known of him, would have known how my father spent his summers, would have known of the man he loved enough to name his firstborn son after.

The story simply was not true. My father had made it up.

Just as my mother's story about Sonny Tufts is not true. Yesterday, when I happened to come across the article about Sonny Tufts from the *Boston Globe*, dated June 8, 1970, and written by the late George Frazier, I wouldn't have bothered to reread it if the week before I had not been joking about Sonny Tufts with a friend, a woman who lives in Boston and whose mother died this past summer. My friend's mother's death, like my father's, was caused by acute alcoholism and had been going on for years. What most suicides accomplish in minutes, my father and my friend's mother took decades to do.

The death of my friend's mother reminded me of the consequences of the death of my father and of my mother's continuing to live. And then our chic joke about the 1940s film star ("Whatever happened to Sonny Tufts?"), a joke about our own aging, reminded me of my mother's story about the senior play in 1932, so that when I saw Frazier's obituary for Tufts, entitled "Death of a Bonesman" (Tufts had gone to Yale and been tapped for Skull and Bones), instead of tossing it back in the drawer or into the wastebasket, I read it through to the end, as if searching for a reference to my mother's having brushed him off. Instead, I learned that Bowen Charlton Tufts III, scion of an old Boston banking family, had prepped for Yale at Exeter. So that his closest connection to the daughter of a machinist in Catamount, and to me, was probably through his father's bank's ownership of the mill where the machinist ran a lathe.

I had never believed the story anyhow, but now I had proof that she made it up. Just as the fact that I have never been interviewed by Dan Rather is proof that my mother never saw me on television in her one-room apartment in San Diego being interviewed by Dan Rather. By the time she got her friend down the hall to come and see her son on TV, Dan had gone on to some depressing stuff about the Middle East.

As for Grace Metalious's characters from *Peyton Place* showing up at a Christmas party in my parents' house in Catamount, I never believed that, either. *Peyton Place* was indeed based on a true story about a young woman's murder of her father in Gilmanton, New Hampshire, a village some twenty-five miles from Catamount, but in the middle 1940s people simply did not drive twenty-five miles over snowcovered back roads on a winter night to go to a party given by strangers.

I said that to my mother. She had just finished telling me, for the hundredth time, it seemed, that someday, based on my own experiences as a child and now as an adult in New

Hampshire, I should be able to write another *Peyton Place*. This was barely two months ago, and I was visiting her in San Diego, an extension of a business trip to Los Angeles, and I was seated rather uncomfortably in her one-room apartment. She is a tiny, wrenlike woman with few possessions, most of which seem miniaturized, designed to fit her small body and the close confines of her room, so that when I visit her I feel huge and oafish. I lower my voice and move with great care.

She was ironing her sheets, while I sat on the unmade sofa bed, unmade because I had just turned the mattress for her, a chore she saves for when I or my younger brother, the only large-sized people in her life now, visits her from the East. "But we *weren't* strangers to them," my mother chirped. "Your father knew the Golden boy somehow. Probably one of his local drinking friends," she said. "Anyhow, that's why your father wouldn't let me tell anyone, after the story came out in the papers, about the murder and the incest and all . . ."

"Incest? What incest?"

"You know, the father who got killed, killed and buried in the manure pile by his own daughter because he'd been committing incest with her. Didn't you read the book?"

"No."

"Well, your father, he was afraid we'd get involved somehow. So I couldn't tell anyone about it until after the book got famous. You know, whenever I tell people out here that back in New Hampshire in the forties I knew the girl who killed her father in *Peyton Place*, they won't believe me. Well, not exactly *knew* her, but you know . . ."

There's always someone famous in her stories, I thought. Dan Rather, Sonny Tufts, Grace Metalious (though my mother can never remember her name, only the name of the book she wrote). It's as if she hopes you will love her more easily if she is associated somehow with fame.

When you know a story isn't true, you think you don't have to listen to it. What you think you're supposed to do is interpret, as I was doing that morning in my mother's room, converting her story into a clue to her psychology, which in turn would lead me to compare it to my own psychology and, with relief, disapprove. (*My* stories don't have famous people in them.) I did the same thing with my father's drunken fiddler, Uncle Earl, once I learned he didn't exist. I used the story as a clue to help unravel the puzzle of my father's dreadful psychology, hoping no doubt to unravel the puzzle of my own.

One of the most difficult things to say to another person is I hope you will love me. Yet that is what we all want to say to one another—to our children, to our parents and mates, to our friends and even to strangers.

Perhaps especially to strangers. My friend in Boston, who joked with me about Sonny Tufts as an interlude in the story of her mother's awful dying, was showing me her hope that I would love her, even when the story itself was about her mother's lifelong refusal to love her and, with the woman's death, the absolute removal of any possibility of that love. I have, at least, my father's story of how I got my name, and though it's too late for me now to give him what, for a glimmering moment, he hoped and asked for, by remembering his story I have understood a little more usefully the telling of my own.

By remembering, as if writing my memoirs, what the stories of others have reminded me of, what they have literally brought to my mind, I have learned how my own stories function in the world, whether I tell them to my mother, to my wife, to my children, to my friends or, especially, to strangers. And to complete the circle, I have learned a little more usefully how to listen to the stories of others, whether they are true or not.

As I was leaving my mother that morning to drive back to Los Angeles and then fly home to New Hampshire, where my brother and sister and all my mother's grandchildren live and where all but the last few years of my mother's past was lived, she told me a new story. We stood in the shade of palm trees in the parking lot outside her glass-and-metal building for a few minutes, and she said to me in a concerned way, "You know that restaurant, the Pancake House, where you took me for breakfast this morning?"

I said yes and checked the time and flipped my suitcase into the back seat of the rented car.

"Well, I always have breakfast there on Wednesdays, it's on the way to where I baby-sit on Wednesdays, and this week something funny happened there. I was alone way in the back, where they have that long, curving booth, and I didn't notice until I was halfway through my breakfast that at the far end of the booth a man was sitting there. He was maybe your age, a young man, but dirty and shabby. Especially dirty, and so I just looked away and went on eating my eggs and toast.

"But then I noticed he was looking at me, as if he knew me and didn't quite dare talk to me. I smiled, because maybe I did know him, I know just about everybody in the neighborhood now. But he was a stranger. And dirty. And I could see that he had been drinking for days.

"So I smiled and said to him, 'You want help, mister, don't you?' He needed a shave, and his clothes were filthy and all ripped, and his hair was a mess. You know the type. But something pathetic about his eyes made me want to talk to him. But honestly, Earl, I couldn't. I just couldn't. He was so dirty and all.

"Anyhow, when I spoke to him, just that little bit, he sort of came out of his daze and sat up straight for a second, like he was afraid I was going to complain to the manager and have him thrown out of the restaurant. 'What did you say to me?' he asked. His voice was weak but he was trying to make it sound strong, so it came out kind of loud and broken. 'Nothing,' I said, and I turned away from him and quickly finished my breakfast and left.

"That afternoon, when I was walking back home from my baby-sitting job, I went into the restaurant to see if he was there, but he wasn't. And the next morning, Thursday, I walked all the way over there to check again, even though I never eat breakfast at the Pancake House on Thursdays, but he was gone then too. And then yesterday, Friday, I went back a third time. But he was gone." She lapsed into a thoughtful silence and looked at her hands.

"Was he there this morning?" I asked, thinking coincidence was somehow the point of the story.

"No," she said. "But I didn't expect him to be there this morning. I'd stopped looking for him by yesterday."

"Well, why'd you tell me the story, then? What's it about?"

"About? Why, I don't know. Nothing, I guess. I just felt sorry for the man, and then because I was afraid, I shut up and left him alone." She was still studying her tiny hands.

"That's natural," I said. "You shouldn't feel guilty for that," I said, and I put my arms around her.

She turned her face into my shoulder. "I know, I know. But still . . ." Her blue eyes filled, her son was leaving again, gone for another six months or a year, and who would she tell her stories to while he was gone? Who would listen?

[1986]

# AND THE 3d
# BIGGEST LIE IS...

## Ann Landers

Dear Readers:
A while back, I was asked to print the three biggest lies in the world. I was able to come up with only two: "I'm from the government and I'm here to help you," and "The check is in the mail."

I asked my readers if they could supply the third biggest lie. Thousands rose to the occasion. The mail was simply wonderful. Here's a sampling:

*From Lebanon, Pa.*: It's a good thing you came in today. We have only two more in stock.

*Wilmington, Del.*: Sorry, dear, not tonight. I have a headache.

*Sparta, Wis.*: I promise to pay you back out of my next paycheck.

*Woodbridge, N.J.*: Five pounds is nothing on a person with your height.

*Harrisburg, Pa.*: But officer, I only had two beers.

*Hammond, Ind.*: You made it yourself? I never would have guessed.

*Baltimore*: Of course I will respect you in the morning.

*Eau Claire, Wis.*: It's delicious, but I can't eat another bite.

*Charlotte, N.C.*: Your hair looks just fine.

*Philadelphia:* It's nothing to worry about—just a cold sore.

*La Palma, Calif.*: I've finished my homework. Now can I read Ann Landers?

*Mechanicsburg, Pa.*: It's a terrific high and I swear you won't get hooked.

*Dallas:* The river never gets high enough to flood this property.

*Manassas, Va.:* The delivery is on the truck.

*Tacoma, Wash.:* Go ahead and tell me. I promise I won't get mad.

*Billings, Mont.:* You have nothing to worry about, honey. I've had a vasectomy.

*Philadelphia:* The three biggest lies: I did it. I didn't do it. I can't remember.

*Chicago:* This car is like brand new. It was owned by two retired schoolteachers who never went anywhere.

*Boston:* The doctor will call you right back.

*Montreal:* So glad you dropped by. I wasn't doing a thing.

**US Stars and Stripes:** You don't look a day over 40.

*Washington, D.C.:* Dad, I need to move out of the dorm into an apartment of my own so I can have some peace and quiet when I study.

*Windsor, Ont.:* It's a very small spot. Nobody will notice.

*Cleveland:* The baby is just beautiful!

*New York:* The new ownership won't affect you. The company will remain the same.

*Holiday, Fla.:* I gave at the office.

*Lansing, Mich.:* You can tell me. I won't breathe a word to a soul.

*Huntsville, Ala.:* The puppy won't be any trouble, Mom. I promise I'll take care of it myself.

*Minneapolis:* I'm a social drinker and I can quit anytime I want to.

*Barrington, Ill.:* Put the map away. I know exactly how to get there.

*Troy, Mich.:* You don't need it in writing. You have my personal guarantee.

*Greenwich, Conn.:* Sorry the work isn't ready. The computer broke down.

*Mexico City:* I'll do it in a minute.

*Elkhart, Ind.*: The reason I'm so late is we ran out of gas.

*Scarsdale, N.Y.*: Our children never caused us a minute's trouble.

*Detroit:* This is a very safe building. No way will you ever be burglarized.

*Glendale, Calif.*: Having a great time. Wish you were here.

[1989]

# LIAR'S POKER

## Michael Lewis

IT WAS SOMETIME EARLY IN 1986, THE FIRST YEAR OF THE decline of my firm, Salomon Brothers. Our chairman, John Gutfreund, left his desk at the head of the trading floor and went for a walk. At any given moment on the trading floor billions of dollars were being risked by bond traders. Gutfreund took the pulse of the place by simply wandering around it and asking questions of the traders. An eerie sixth sense guided him to wherever a crisis was unfolding. Gutfreund seemed able to smell money being lost.

He was the last person a nerve-racked trader wanted to see. Gutfreund (pronounced *Good friend*) liked to sneak up from behind and surprise you. This was fun for him but not for you. Busy on two phones at once trying to stem disaster, you had no time to turn and look. You didn't need to. You felt him. The area around you began to convulse like an epileptic ward. People were pretending to be frantically busy and at the same time staring intently at a spot directly above your head. You felt a chill in your bones that I imagine belongs to the same class of intelligence as the nervous twitch of a small furry animal at the silent approach of a grizzly bear. An alarm shrieked in your head: Gutfreund! Gutfreund! Gutfreund!

Often as not, our chairman just hovered quietly for a bit, then left. You might never have seen him. The only trace I found of him on two of these occasions was a turdlike ash on the floor beside my chair, left, I suppose, as a calling card. Gutfreund's cigar droppings were longer and better formed than those of the average Salomon boss. I always assumed that he smoked a more expensive blend than the rest, purchased with a few of the $40 million he had cleared on the sale of Salomon Brothers in 1981 (or a few of the $3.1 million he paid himself in 1986, more than any other Wall Street CEO).

This day in 1986, however, Gutfreund did something strange. Instead of terrifying us all, he walked a straight line to the trading desk of John Meriwether, a member of the board of Salomon Inc. and also one of Salomon's finest bond traders. He whispered a few words. The traders in the vicinity eavesdropped. What Gutfreund said has become a legend at Salomon Brothers and a visceral part of its corporate identity. He said: "One hand, one million dollars, no tears."

One hand, one million dollars, no tears. Meriwether grabbed the meaning instantly. The King of Wall Street, as *Business Week* had dubbed Gutfreund, wanted to play a single hand of a game called Liar's Poker for a million dollars. He played the game most afternoons with Meriwether and the six young bond arbitrage traders who worked for Meriwether and was usually skinned alive. Some traders said Gutfreund was heavily outmatched. Others who couldn't imagine John Gutfreund as anything but omnipotent—and there were many—said that losing suited his purpose, though exactly what that might be was a mystery.

The peculiar feature of Gutfreund's challenge this time was the size of the stake. Normally his bets didn't exceed a few hundred dollars. A million was unheard of. The final two words of his challenge, "no tears," meant that the loser was expected to suffer a great deal of pain but wasn't entitled to whine, bitch, or moan about it. He'd just have to hunker down and keep his poverty to himself. But why? You might ask if you were anyone other than the King of Wall Street. Why do it in the first place? Why, in particular, challenge Meriwether instead of some lesser managing director? It seemed an act of sheer lunacy. Meriwether was the King of the Game, the Liar's Poker champion of the Salomon Brothers trading floor.

On the other hand, one thing you learn on a trading floor is that winners like Gutfreund *always* have some reason for what they do; it might not be the best of reasons, but at least they have a concept in mind. I was not privy to Gutfreund's innermost thoughts, but I do know that all the boys on the trading floor gambled and that he wanted badly to be one of the boys. What I think Gutfreund had in mind in this instance was a desire to show his courage, like the boy who leaps from the high dive. Who better than Meriwether for the purpose? Besides, Meriwether was probably the only trader with both the cash and the nerve to play.

The whole absurd situation needs putting into context. John Meriwether had, in the course of his career, made hundreds of millions of dollars for Salomon Brothers. He had an ability, rare among people and treasured by traders, to hide his state of mind. Most traders divulge whether they are making or losing money by the way they speak or move. They are either overly easy or overly tense. With Meriwether you could never, ever tell. He wore the same blank half-tense expression when he won as he did when he lost. He had, I think, a profound ability to control the two emotions that commonly destroy traders—fear and greed—and it made him as noble as a man who pursues his self-interest so fiercely can be. He was thought by many within Salomon to be the best bond trader on Wall Street. Around Salomon no tone but awe was used when he was discussed. People would say, "He's the best businessman in the place," or "the best risk taker I have ever seen," or "a very dangerous Liar's Poker player."

Meriwether cast a spell over the young traders who worked for him. His boys ranged in age from twenty-five to thirty-two (he was about forty). Most of them had Ph.D.'s in math, economics, and/or physics. Once they got onto Meriwether's trading desk, however, they forgot they were supposed to be detached intellectuals. They became disciples.

They became obsessed by the game of Liar's Poker. They regarded it as *their* game. And they took it to a new level of seriousness.

John Gutfreund was always the outsider in their game. That *Business Week* put his picture on the cover and called him the King of Wall Street held little significance for them. I mean, that was, in a way, the whole point. Gutfreund was the King of Wall Street, but Meriwether was King of the Game. When Gutfreund had been crowned by the gentlemen of the press, you could almost hear traders thinking: *Foolish names and foolish faces often appear in public places.* Fair enough, Gutfreund had once been a trader, but that was as relevant as an old woman's claim that she was once quite a dish.

At times Gutfreund himself seemed to agree. He loved to trade. Compared with managing, trading was admirably direct. You made your bets and either you won or you lost. When you won, people—all the way up to the top of the firm—admired you, envied you, and feared you, and with reason: You controlled the loot. When you managed a firm, well, sure you received your quota of envy, fear, and admiration. But for all the wrong reasons. *You did not make the money for Salomon. You did not take risk.* You were hostage to your producers. They took risk. They proved their superiority every day by handling risk better than the rest of the risk-taking world. The money came from risk takers such as Meriwether, and whether it came or not was really beyond Gutfreund's control. That's why many people thought that the single rash act of challenging the arbitrage boss to one hand for a million dollars was Gutfreund's way of showing he was a player, too. And if you wanted to show off, Liar's Poker was the only way to go. The game had a powerful meaning for traders. People like John Meriwether believed that Liar's Poker had a lot in common with bond trading. It tested a trader's character. It honed a trader's instincts. A good player made a good trader, and vice versa. We all understood it.

The Game: In Liar's Poker a group of people—as few as two, as many as ten—form a circle. Each player holds a dollar bill close to his chest. The game is similar in spirit to the card game known as I Doubt It. Each player attempts to fool the others about the serial numbers printed on the face of his dollar bill. One trader begins by making "a bid." He says, for example, "Three sixes." He means that all told the serial numbers of the dollar bills held by every player, including himself, contain at least three sixes.

Once the first bid has been made, the game moves clockwise in the circle. Let's say the bid is three sixes. The player to the left of the bidder can do one of two things. He can bid higher (there are two sorts of higher bids: the same quantity of a higher number [three sevens, eights, or nines] and more of any number [four fives, for instance]). Or he can "challenge"—that is like saying, "I doubt it."

The bidding escalates until all the other players agree to challenge a single player's bid. Then, and only then, do the players reveal their serial numbers and determine who is bluffing whom. In the midst of all this, the mind of a good player spins with probabilities. What is the statistical likelihood of there being three sixes within a batch of, say, forty randomly generated serial numbers? For a great player, however, the math is the easy part of the game. The hard part is reading the faces of the other players. The complexity arises when all players know how to bluff and double-bluff.

The game has some of the feel of trading, just as jousting has some of the feel of war. The questions a Liar's Poker player asks himself are, up to a point, the same questions a bond trader asks himself. Is this a smart risk? Do I feel lucky? How cunning is my opponent? Does he have any idea what he's doing, and if not, how do I exploit his ignorance? If he bids high, is he bluffing, or does he actually hold a strong hand? Is he trying to induce me to make a foolish bid, or does he actually have four of a kind himself? Each player seeks weakness, predictability, and pattern in the others and seeks to avoid it in himself. The bond traders of Goldman, Sachs, First Boston, Morgan Stanley, Merrill Lynch, and other Wall Street firms all play some version of Liar's Poker. But the place where the stakes run highest, thanks to John Meriwether, is the New York bond trading floor of Salomon Brothers.

The code of the Liar's Poker player was something like the code of the gunslinger. It required a trader to accept all challenges. Because of the code—which was *his* code—John Meriwether felt obliged to play. But he knew it was stupid. For him, there was no upside. If he won, he upset Gutfreund. No good came of this. But if he lost, he was out of pocket a million bucks. This was worse than upsetting the boss. Although Meriwether was by far the better player of the game, in a single hand anything could happen. Luck could very well determine the outcome. Meriwether spent his entire day avoiding dumb bets, and he wasn't about to accept this one.

"No, John," he said, "if we're going to play for those kind of numbers, I'd rather play for real money. Ten million dollars. No tears."

*Ten million dollars.* It was a moment for all players to savor. Meriwether was playing Liar's Poker before the game even started. He was bluffing. Gutfreund considered the counterproposal. It would have been just like him to accept. Merely to entertain the thought was a luxury that must have pleased him well. (It *was* good to be rich.)

On the other hand, ten million dollars was, and is, a lot of money. If Gutfreund lost, he'd have only thirty million or so left. His wife, Susan, was busy spending the better part of fifteen million dollars redecorating their Manhattan apartment (Meriwether knew this). And as Gutfreund *was* the boss, he clearly wasn't bound by the Meriwether code. Who knows? Maybe he didn't even know the Meriwether code. Maybe the whole point of his challenge was to judge Meriwether's response. (Even Gutfreund had to marvel at the king in action.) So Gutfreund declined. In fact, he smiled his own brand of forced smile and said, "You're crazy."

No, thought Meriwether, just very, very good.

[1989]

# THE DUKE OF DECEPTION

## Geoffrey Wolff

DUKE CHARGED AHEAD. HE CHARGED AND CHARGED AHEAD.
There was something about him, what he wanted he got.
Salesmen loved him, he was the highest evolution of con-
sumer. Discriminating, too: he railed against shoddy goods and
cheapjack workmanship. He would actually return, for credit,
an electric blender or an alpine tent that didn't perform, by his
lights, to specification. He demanded the best and never mind
the price. As for debts, they didn't bother him at all. He said
that merchants who were owed stayed on their toes, aimed to
please. Dunning letters meant nothing to him. He laughed off
the vulgar thrustings of the book and record clubs, with their
absurd threats to take him to law. People owed a bundle, who
brought out their heavy artillery, got my father's Samuel
Johnson remark: "Small debts are like small shot; they are rat-
tling on every side, and can scarcely be escaped without
wound; great debts are like cannon, of loud noise but little
danger." He was slippery: he used the telephone to persuade
the telephone company he should be allowed a sixth month of
non-payment without suffering disconnection, because he
needed to call people long distance to borrow money from
them to pay his telephone bills. He was cool, but not icy. He
owed a Westport barkeep a couple of hundred, and when the
man died in a car accident my father was sorry, and told his
widow about the debt, not that he ever paid her.

Finally it got out of hand. It has nowhere to go but out of
hand. I wearied of telling people on our stoop or through the
phone that they had the wrong Arthur Wolff, that my father
had just left for the hospital, or the Vale of Kashmir, or Quito.

I tired of asking "How do I know you're who you say you are?" when people asked questions about my father's whereabouts and plans. I hated it, wanted to flee. It was October; there were months still to get through, too many months but too few to cobble up a miracle of loaves and find the twenty-five hundred dollars to buy my way back into Princeton.

. . .

My father and I were watching the Giants play the Colts in the snow for the championship when two Connecticut State troopers arrived during the first sudden death overtime. They watched with us till the game ended, and then took my father to the lockup in Danbury. He had left a bad check at The Three Bears; they were pressing charges. I found a mouthpiece who went bail, made good the check and got the charges dropped. Duke had talked with him. The old man hadn't lost his touch at all, only with me. With me he had lost his touch.

A week before my birthday he wrecked my Delahaye. I loved the dumb car. I was in bed when I heard him climb the driveway cursing. He was blind drunk, drunker than I'd ever seen him. He railed at me as soon as he came in, called me a phony. I feigned sleep, he burst through the room, blinded me with the overhead light, told me I was full of crap, a zero, zed, cipher, blanko, double-zero.

"I'm leaving you," he said.

I laughed: "In what?"

A mistake. His face reddened. I sat up, pretending to rub sleep from my eyes while he swore at my car, said it had damned near killed him swerving into the ditch, it could rot there for all he cared. He was usually just a finger-wagger, but I still feared him. Now he poked my bare chest with his stiff yellow finger, for punctuation. It hurt. I was afraid. Then I wasn't afraid; I came off my bed naked, cocked my fist at my father, and said: "Leave me alone."

My father moved fast to his room, shut the door, and

locked it. I was astounded. I don't believe he was afraid of me;
I believe he was afraid of what he might do to me. I sat on the
edge of my bed, shaking with anger. He turned on his television set loud: Jack Paar. He hated Paar. There was a shot, a
hollow noise from the .45. I had heard that deep awful boom
before, coming from the black cellar in Birmingham, a bedroom in Saybrook. I thought my father would kill me. That
was my first thought. Then that he would kill himself, then
that he had already killed himself. I heard it again, again,
again. He raged, glass broke, again, again. The whole clip.
Nothing. Silence from him, silence from Paar. A low moan,
laughter rising to a crescendo, breaking, a howl, sobs, more
laughter. I called to my father.

"Shit fire," he answered, "now I've done it, now I've *done* it!"

He had broken. No police, the phone was finally discon-
nected. I tried the door. Locked. Shook it hard. Locked fast. I
moved back to shoulder through and as in a comic movie, it
opened.

My father had shot out Jack Paar; bits of tubes and wires
were strewn across the floor. He had shot out the pretty water-
colors painted by Betty during their Mississippi rendezvous. He
had shot out himself in the mirror. Behind the mirror was his
closet, and he was looking into his closet at his suits. Dozens of
bespoke suits, symmetrically hung, and through each suit a
couple of holes in both pant-legs, a couple in the jacket. Four
holes at least in each suit, six in the vested models.

"Hell of a weapon," my father said.

"Oh, yes," I said. "*Hell* of a weapon!"

November fifth I turned twenty-one. My father had a present
for me, two presents really, a present and its wrappings. He
gave me his gold signet ring, the one I wear today—lions and
fleurs-de-lis *nulla vesligium retrorsit*—wrapped in a scrap of
white paper, a due bill signed *Dad*, witnessed and notarized by
a Danbury real estate agent: *I.O.U. Princeton.*

"How?" I asked.

"Piece of cake," my father said, "done and done."

I was due at Princeton January 15th. By then the Abarth had been repossessed and the Delahaye was still and forever a junker. I rode to Sikorsky with Nick, who drove twenty miles out of his way to pick me up and return me in his Edsel. After work the day following New Year's I found a rented black Buick in the driveway. My father told me to help him pack it, we were leaving pronto and for good; what didn't come with us we'd never see again. I asked questions. I got no answers, except this:

"It's Princeton time. We're going by way of Boston."

I almost believed him. We packed, walked away from everything. I wish I had the stuff now, letters, photographs, a Boy Scout merit badge sash, Shep's ribbon; *Gentlest in Show* at the Old Lyme grade school fair. My father had had his two favorite suits rewoven; he left the rest behind with most of his shoes, umbrellas, hats, accessories. He left behind the model Bentley that cost him half a year to build. He brought his camera, the little Minox he always carried and never used ("handy if someone whacks you with his car, here's the old evidence machine," he'd say, tapping the silly chain on the silly camera). I brought my typewriter and my novel. While my father had watched television, I had written a novel. I worked on it every night, with my bedroom door shut; my father treated it like a rival, which it was, a still, invented place safe from him. He made cracks about The Great Book, and resented me for locking it away every night when I finished with it, while he shut down the Late Show, and then the Late Late. I made much of not showing it to him.

On the way to Boston we stopped by Stratford, where Sikorsky had moved. I quit, told the personnel department where to send my final check, said goodbye to no one. When I returned to the car my father said to me:

"Fiction is the thing for you. Finish Princeton if you want, but don't let them turn you into a goddamned professor or a critic. Write make-believe. You've got a feel for it."

Had he read my stuff? "Why, do you think?"

"I know you."

We drove directly to Shreve, Crump & Low, Boston's finest silversmith. Duke double-parked on Boylston Street and asked me to help him unload two canvas duffels from the trunk. He called them "parachute bags"; maybe that's what they were, parachute bags. They were heavy as corpses; we had to share the load.

"What's going on?" I asked. "What's in here?"

"Never mind. Help me."

We sweated the bags into the store, past staring ladies and gentlemen to the manager. My father opened a zipper and there was Alice's flat silver: solid silver gun-handle knives, instruments to cut fish and lettuce, dessert spoons and lobster forks, three-tined forks and four-tined forks, every imaginable implement, service for sixteen. In the other bag were teapots, coffeepots, creamers, saltcellars, Georgian treasure, the works polished by my father, piles gleaming dangerously in the lumpy canvas sacks.

The manager examined a few pieces. He was correct; he looked from my face to my father's while he spoke.

"These are very nice, as you know. I could perhaps arrange a buyer . . . This will take time. If you're in no rush . . ."

"I want money today," my father said.

"This will be quite impossible," the manager said.

"I won't quibble," my father said. "I know what the silver is worth, but I'm pinched, I won't quibble."

"You don't understand," the manager said.

"Let's not play games," my father said.

"This is quite impossible," the manager said. "I think you'd best take this all away now."

"Won't you make an offer?"

"No," the manager said.

"Nothing?" my father asked.

"Nothing."

"You're a fool," my father told the manager of Shreve, Crump & Low.

"I think not," said the manager of Shreve, Crump & Low. "Good afternoon, gentlemen."

We reloaded the car. I said nothing to my father, and he said nothing to me. There we were. It was simple, really, where everything had been pointing, right over the line. This wasn't mischief. This wouldn't make a funny story back among my college pals. This was something else. We drove to a different kind of place. This one had cages on the windows, and the neighborhood wasn't good. The manager here was also different.

"You want to pawn all this stuff?"

"Yes," my father said.

"Can you prove ownership?"

"Yes."

"Okay," the pawnbroker said. He sorted through it, scratched a few pieces and touched them with a chemical.

"It's solid silver," my father said.

"Yes," the man said, "it is."

"What will you loan us, about?"

I heard the *us*. I looked straight at my father, and he looked straight back.

"Will you reclaim it soon?" My father shrugged at this question. "Because if you don't really need it, if you'd sell it, I'd buy. We're talking about more money now, about four times what I'd loan you."

"What would you do with it?" my father asked. "Sell it?"

"No," the man said. "I'd melt it down."

My father looked at me: "Okay?"

"Okay," I said.

My father nodded. While he signed something the man took cash from a huge floor safe. He counted it out, twenties bound in units of five hundred dollars. I looked away, didn't want to know the bottom line on this one. There were limits, for me, I thought.

We checked into the Ritz-Carlton. Looked at each other and smiled. I felt all right, pretty good, great. I felt great.

"What now?" I asked my father.

Years later I read about the Philadelphia cobbler and his twelve-year-old son said to have done such awful things together, robbing at first, breaking and entering. Then much worse, rape and murder. I wondered if it could have kept screwing tighter that way for us, higher stakes, lower threshold of *this, but not that*. I thought that day in the Ritz, sun setting, that we might wind up with girls, together in the same room with a couple of girls. But as in Seattle I had misread my father.

"Let's get some champers and fish-eggs up here," he said.

So we drank Dom Perignon and ate Beluga caviar and watched night fall over Boston Common. Then we took dinner at Joseph's and listened to Teddy Wilson play piano at Mahogany Hall. Back at the Ritz, lying in clean linen in the quiet room, my father shared with me a scheme he had been a long time hatching.

"Here's how it works. I think I can make this work, I'm sure I can. Here's how it goes. Okay, I go to a medium-size town, check into a hotel, not the worst, not the best. I open an account at the local bank, cash a few small checks, give them time to clear. I go to a Cadillac showroom just before closing on Friday, point to the first car I see and say I'll buy it, no road test or questions, no haggling."

My father spoke deliberately, doing both voices in the dark. When he spoke as an ingratiating salesman he flattened his accent, and didn't stammer:

"How would you care to pay, sir? Will you be financing

your purchase? Do you want to trade in your present automobile?"

"This is a cash purchase. (The salesman beams.) I'm paying
by check. (The salesman frowns a little.) On a local bank, of
course. (The salesman beams again.)"

"Fine, sir. We'll have the car registered and cleaned. It'll be
ready Monday afternoon."

"At this I bristle. I bristle well, don't you think?"

"You are probably the sovereign bristler of our epoch," I
told my father.

He would tell the saleman he wanted the car now or not at
all, period. There would be a nervous conference, beyond my
father's hearing, with the dealer. The dealer would note Duke's
fine clothes and confident bearing; now or never was this customer's way, *carpe diem*, here was an *easy* sale, car leaving town,
maybe just maybe this was kosher. Probably not, but how many
top-of-the-line cars can you sell right off the floor, no bullshit
about price, color, or options? Now the dealer was in charge,
the salesman wasn't man enough for this decision. The dealer
would telephone Duke's hotel and receive lukewarm assur-
ances. Trembling, plunging, he would take Duke's check. My
father would drive to a used car dealer a block or two away,
offer to sell his fine new automobile for whatever he was
offered, he was in a rush, yeah, three thousand was okay. A
telephone call would be made to the dealer. Police would
arrive. My father would protest his innocence, spend the weekend in a cell. Monday the check would clear. Tuesday my
father would retain the services of a shyster, if the dealer hadn't
already settled. With the police he would never settle. False
arrest would put him on Easy Street. How did I like it?

"Nice sting. It might work." The Novice.

"Or course it will work." The Expert.

The next morning we checked out and my father mailed the
Buick's keys to a Hertz agent in Stamford, telling him where

to find his car. Then a VW bus materialized. My father had taken it for a test drive; maybe he paid for it later, and maybe he forgot to pay for it later. My father called this "freeloading."

We drove to Princeton in the bus, with my novel on the back seat beside a cooler filled with cracked ice and champagne, a cash purchase from S.S. Pierce. We reached Princeton about four and parked on Nassau Street, outside the Annex Grill, across from Firestone Library.

"How much did you give me last year?"

"About twenty-five hundred," I said, "but a lot of that was for my own keep."

"I don't charge my boy room and board," my father said. He pulled clumps of twenties from a manila envelope. Five packets, twenty-five hundred dollars, there it was, every penny, just as he had promised, precisely what I owed. "And here's another five hundred to get you started."

"Thanks," I said. "Where will you go now?"

"New York for a while. Then, I don't know. Maybe California. I always had luck in California."

"Sounds like a good plan," I said. "Stay in touch," I said.

"Sure," he said. "Do well, Geoffrey. Be good."

"Sure," I said. "I won't screw up this time."

"No, he said, "you probably won't. Now don't be *too* good. There's such a thing as too good."

"Don't worry," I said laughing, wanting this to end.

"Don't forget your book," my father said, while I unloaded the van. "I'll be reading it someday, I guess. I'll be in touch, you'll hear from me, hang in there."

He was gone. An illegal turn on Nassau headed him back where he had come from.

[1979]

# WHO STOLE MY GOLDEN METAPHOR?

## S. J. Perelman

I HAD A SUIT OVER MY ARM AND WAS HEADING WEST DOWN Eighth Street, debating whether to take it to one of those 24-hour dry-cleaning establishments or a Same-Day Cleaner or even a place that might return it before I left it, when I ran smack into Vernon Equinox in front of the Waffle Shop. Fair weather or foul, Vernon can usually be found along there between MacDougal Street and Sixth Avenue, scanning the bargain Jung in the corner bookshop or disparaging the fake Negro primitive masks at the stationery store. His gaunt, greenish-white face, edged in the whiskers once characteristic of fisherfolk and stage Irishmen and now favored by Existentialist poets, his dungarees flecked with paint, and his huaraches and massive turquise rings clearly stamp Vernon as a practitioner of the arts, though which one is doubtful. The fact is that he favors them all impartially. He writes an occasional diatribe for magazines called *Neurotica* and *Ichor*, paints violent canvases portraying one's sensations under mescaline, dabbles in wire sculpture, and composes music for abstract films as yet unphotographed. He derives his sustenance, if any, from a miniscule shop on Christopher Street, where he designs and fashions copper sconces and jewelry, but since the place is open only from six-thirty in the evening until eight, its revenue is nominal. It has been whispered, late at night in Alex's Borsch Bowl, that Vernon holds a Black Mass now and again in his shop. How he can get a naked woman and a goat into that tiny store, though—let alone himself—is a puzzle.

Anyway, there he was outside the Waffle, staring at the three rows of Dolly Madison ice-cream cones slowly revolving in the window before a background of prisms, and his contempt was magnificent to behold. It was a pretty unnerving display, actually; the ice cream was so obviously pink-tinted cotton and the cones themselves made of the plywood used in orange crates that you intinctively shuddered at the oral damage they could inflict. As he turned away from the window with an almost audible snarl, Vernon caught sight of me.

"Look there," he said furiously, pointing at the multiple rosy reflections shimmering in the glass. "That's what you're up against. Is it any wonder Modigliani died at thirty-three?" I stood transfixed, seeking to fathom the connection between Dolly Madison and the ill-starred Italian painter, but Vernon had already hurdled his rhetorical question. "I give up! I throw in the towel!" he proclaimed. "You spend your whole life trying to imprison a moment of beauty, and they go for borax like that. Gad!"

"When did you get back?" I asked placatingly. There was nothing in his appearance to indicate that he had been away at all, or even exposed to direct sunlight for the past six months; still, it seemed a reasonably safe gambit.

"End of January," he said with a morose backward look at the window.

"Er—how did you like Haiti?" I asked. That too was a wild stab, but I dimly remembered being waylaid outside the Bamboo Forest in an icy wind and told of up-country voodoo rites.

"Haiti?" Vernon repeated, with such withering scorn that two passers-by veered toward the curb. "That tourist drop? Nobody goes there any more. I was in Oaxaca. Not Oaxaca proper, mind you," he corrected, anxious to scotch the impression that he frequented resorts, "a tiny village about sixty miles north, San Juan Doloroso. Completely unspoiled— Elspeth and I lived there for three pesos a day."

"Oh, yes," I said fluently. "Henry Miller mentions it in *Tropic of Capricorn*." From the quick look Vernon gave me, I knew I had planted the seeds of a sleepless night. "Well, old boy," I inquired, giving his shoulder an encouraging clap, "what are you up to these days? When are we going to see a show of those nereids made out of pipe-cleaners?"

"I'm through with that dilettante stuff," said Vernon. "I've been designing some nonobjective puppets. It's a combination of dance and mime. Schoenberg wants to do the music."

"I'd let him," I recommended. "It sounds exciting. Tip me off before the recital, won't you?"

"There isn't going to be any," he said. "The puppets are suspended in zones of light and the music comes over. That is, it's superimposed. We're trying to establish a mood."

"Very definitely," I agreed. "I'm sure it'll work out. Well good luck, and—"

"I'd have finished it months ago if Truman Capote hadn't sabotaged me," Vernon went on irascibly. "The aggravation I suffered from that episode—well, never mind. Why burden you?"

Arrested by the bitterness in his tone, I turned back. "What do you mean?" I asked. "What did he do?"

"Come in here and I'll show you," said Vernon, propelling me into a coffeepot a few doors away. After extensive byplay with the counterman involving the preparation of a muffin, obviously calculated to heighten the suspense, he drew a clipping from his wallet. "Did you read this interview with Capote by Harvey Breit? It came out in the *Times Book Review* around a year ago."

"Why, yes," I said vaguely, scanning the text. "It was rather tiptoe, but then, most of the publicity about him is. I didn't notice anything special."

"Nothing except that the little creep helped himself to my whole style," said Vernon with rancor. "Things I said at different parties. It's the most barefaced—"

"Wait a minute," I interrupted. "Those are blunt words, neighbor. You sure of your facts?"

"Ha *ha!*" Vernon emitted a savage cackle. "I just happen to have about two hundred witnesses, that's all! People who were there! Look at this, for instance." He ran his forefinger down a column. "Breit asked Capote to describe himself, and what do you think he said? 'I'm about as tall as a shotgun—and just as noisy. I think I have rather heated eyes'."

"He's rumored to have ball-and-claw feet too, like a Queen Anne dresser," I returned, "but why should *you* get worked up?"

"Because it's a straight paraphrase of a thumbnail sketch I gave of myself," said Vernon tigerishly. "You know Robin Nankivel, the ceramist—the girl who does the caricatures in porcelain? Well, it was in her studio, next to the Cherry Lane Theater. I remember the whole thing plainly. They were all milling around Capote, making a big fuss. He was wearing a chameleon silk vest and blue tennis sneakers; I could draw you a picture of him. Arpad Fustian, the rug-chandler, and Polly Entrail and I were over in a corner, discussing how we visualized ourselves, and I said I was about as tall as an Osage bow and just as relentless. Right then I happened to look over, and there was Capote looking at me."

"I guess his eyes *are* really heated, though," I said. "The only time I ever saw him, in the balcony of Loew's Valencia, they glowed in the dark like a carnation."

"At first," continued Vernon, too full of his grievance to encompass anything outside it, "I didn't associate this puling little simile of his with my remark. But after I read on further, where he analyzes his voice and features for Breit, I nearly dropped dead. My entire idiom! The same unique, highly individual way I express myself! Here it is—the end of the paragraph. 'Let's see,' he (Capote) said. 'I have a very sassy voice. I like my nose but you can't see it because I wear these thick glasses. If you looked at my face from both sides, you'd see they were completely different. (Mr. Capote demonstrated.) It's sort of a changeling face.'"

I studied the photograph imbedded in the letterpress. "A changeling," I said, thinking out loud, "is a child supposed to have been secretly substituted for another by elves. Does he mean he's not really Truman Capote?"

"Of course he is," said Vernon irritably, "but read the rest——"

"Hold on," I said. "We may have uncovered something pretty peculiar here. This party admits in so many words that he's not legit. How do we know that he hasn't done away with the real Capote—dissolved him in corrosive sublimate or buried him under a floor someplace—and is impersonating him? He's certainly talking funny."

"God damn it, let me finish, will you?" Vernon implored. "It's this last part where he copied my stuff bodily. Listen: 'Do you want to know the real reason why I push my hair down on my forehead? Because I have two cowlicks. If I didn't push my hair forward it would make me look as though I had two feathery horns'."

"Great Scott!" I exclaimed, a light suddenly dawning. "Don't you see who's talking? It's not Capote at all—it's *Pan*. The feathery horns, the ball-and-claw feet—it all ties together!"

"He can be the Grand Mufti of Jerusalem for all I care," snapped Vernon. "All it know is that I was having brunch at Lee Chumley's one Sunday with Karen Nudnic, the choreographer, and she was wearing a bang. I said she looked like one of those impish little satyrs of Aubrey Beardsley's, and that just for kicks she ought to do up her hair in points to accentuate it. Well, I don't have to tell you who was in the next booth with his ear flapping. Of course, I never thought anything of it at the time."

"It's open and shut," I said. "The jury wouldn't even leave the box."

"Ah, why sue a guy like that?" he replied disgustedly. "So I'd expose him publicly and get six cents in damages. Would that recompense me for my humiliation?"

I tried not to appear obtuse, but the odds were against me. "I don't quite understand how he hurt you," I said. "Did any of your friends spot this—er—similarity between Capote's dialogue and your own?"

"No-o-o, not until I wised them up," admitted Vernon.

"Well, did they avoid you subsequently, or did you lose any customers as a result of it?"

"*What?*" he shouted. "You think that twirp could make the slightest difference in my life? You must have a lousy opinion of my—"

"Hey, you in the back!" sang out the counterman. "Pipe down! This ain't Webster Hall!"

"No, and it's not Voisin's either!" Vernon snarled. "The coffee here's pure slop. Who are you paying off down at the Board of Health?"

As the two of them, spitting like tomcats, converged from opposite ends of the bar and joyfully began exchanging abuse, I recovered my suit and squirmed out into Eighth Street. The Dolly Madison cones were still revolving turgidly in the Waffle Shop, and a light spring rain fell on the just and the unjust alike. All at once, the fatuity of dry-cleaning a garment that would only become soiled again overcame me. How much more sensible to put the money into some sound cultural investment, such as a copy of *Other Voices, Other Rooms*, for instance, thereby enriching both its talented author and one's own psyche. I instantly directed my steps toward the corner bookshop, but as luck would have it, halfway there I ran into young bard I know named T. S. Heliogabalus. The story that kid told me!

[1957]

# THEFT

## Katherine Anne Porter

SHE HAD THE PURSE IN HER HAND WHEN SHE CAME IN.
Standing in the middle of the floor, holding her bathrobe
around her and trailing a damp towel in one hand, she sur-
veyed the immediate past and remembered everything clearly.
Yes, she had opened the flap and spread it out on the bench
after she had dried the purse with her handkerchief.

She had intended to take the Elevated, and naturally she
looked in her purse to make certain she had the fare, and was
pleased to find forty cents in the coin envelope. She was going
to pay her own fare, too, even if Camilo did have the habit of
seeing her up the steps and dropping a nickel in the machine
before he gave the turnstile a little push and sent her through
it with a bow. Camilo by a series of compromises had managed to make effective a fairly complete set of smaller courte-
sies, ignoring the larger and more troublesome ones. She had
walked with him to the station in a pouring rain, because she
knew he was almost as poor as she was, and when he insisted
on a taxi, she was firm and said, "You know it simply will not
do." He was wearing a new hat of a pretty biscuit shade, for it
never occurred to him to buy anything of a practical color; he
had put it on for the first time and the rain was spoiling it. She
kept thinking, "But this is dreadful, where will he get another?"
She compared it with Eddie's hats that always seemed to be
precisely seven years old and as if they had been quite pur-
posely left out in the rain, and yet they sat with a careless and
incidental rightness on Eddie. But Camilo was far different; if
he wore a shabby hat it would be merely shabby on him, and

he would lose his spirits over it. If she had not feared Camilo would take it badly, for he insisted on the practice of his little ceremonies up to the point he had fixed for them, she would have said to him as they left Thora's house, "Do go home. I can surely reach the station by myself."

"It is written that we must be rained upon tonight," said Camilo, "so let it be together."

At the foot of the platform stairway she staggered slightly—they were both nicely set up on Thora's cocktails—and said: "At least, Camilo, do me the favor not to climb these stairs in your present state, since for you it is only a matter of coming down again at once, and you'll certainly break your neck."

He made three quick bows, he was Spanish, and leaped off through the rainy darkness. She stood watching him, for he was a very graceful young man, thinking that tomorrow morning he would gaze soberly at his spoiled hat and soggy shoes and possibly associate her with his misery. As she watched, he stopped at the far corner and took off his hat and hid it under his overcoat. She felt she had betrayed him by seeing, because he would have been humiliated if he thought she even suspected him of trying to save his hat.

Roger's voice sounded over her shoulder above the clang of the rain falling on the stairway shed, wanting to know what she was doing out in the rain at this time of night, and did she take herself for a duck? His long, imperturbable face was streaming with water, and he tapped a bulging spot on the breast of his buttoned-up overcoat: "Hat," he said. "Come on, let's take a taxi."

She settled back against Roger's arm which he laid around her shoulders, and with the gesture they exchanged a glance full of long amiable associations, then she looked through the window at the rain changing the shapes of everything, and the colors. The taxi dodged in and out between the pillars of the Elevated, skidding slightly on every curve, and she said: "The more it skids the calmer I feel, so I really must be drunk."

"You must be," said Roger. "This bird is a homicidal maniac, and I could do with a cocktail myself this minute."

They waited on the traffic at Fortieth Street and Sixth Avenue, and three boys walked before the nose of the taxi. Under the globes of light they were cheerful scarecrows, all very thin and all wearing very seedy snappy-cut suits and gay neckties. They were not very sober either, and they stood for a moment wobbling in front of the car, and there was an argument going on among them. They leaned toward each other as if they were getting ready to sing, and the first one said: "When I get married it won't be jus' for getting married, I'm gonna marry for *love*, see?" and the second one said, "Aw, gwan and tell that stuff to *her*, why n't yuh?" and the third one gave a kind of hoot, and said, "Hell, dis guy? Wot the hell's he got?" and the first one said: "Aaah, shurrup yuh mush, I got plenty." Then they all squealed and scrambled across the street beating the first one on the back and pushing him around.

"Nuts," commented Roger, "pure nuts."

Two girls went skittering by in short transparent raincoats, one green, one red, their heads tucked against the drive of the rain. One of them was saying to the other, "Yes, I know all about *that*. But what about me? You're always so sorry for *him* . . . " and they ran on with their little pelican legs flashing back and forth.

The taxi backed up suddenly and leaped forward again, and after a while Roger said: "I had a letter from Stella today, and she'll be home on the twenty-sixth, so I suppose she's made up her mind and it's all settled."

"I had a sort of letter today too," she said, "making up my mind for me. I think it is time for you and Stella to do something definite."

When the taxi stopped on the corner of West Fifty-third Street, Roger said, "I've just enough if you'll add ten cents," so she opened her purse and gave him a dime, and he said, "That's beautiful, that purse."

"It's a birthday present," she told him, "and I like it. How's
your show coming?"

"Oh, still hanging on, I guess. I don't go near the place.
Nothing sold yet. I mean to keep right on the way I'm going
and they can take it or leave it. I'm through with the argument."

"It's absolutely a matter of holding out, isn't it?"

"Holding out's the tough part."

"Good night, Roger."

"Good night, you should take aspirin and push youself into
a tub of hot water, you look as though you're catching cold."

"I will."

With the purse under her arm she went upstairs, and on
the first landing Bill heard her step and poked his head out
with his hair tumbled and his eyes red, and he said: "For
Christ's sake, come in and have a drink with me. I've had
some bad news."

"You're perfectly sopping," said Bill, looking at her
drenched feet. They had two drinks, while Bill told how the
director had thrown his play out after the cast had been
picked over twice, and had gone through three rehearsals. "I
said to him, 'I didn't say it was a masterpiece, I said it would
make a good show.' And he said, 'It just doesn't *play*, do you
see? It needs a doctor.' So I'm stuck, absolutely stuck," said
Bill, on the edge of weeping again. "I've been crying," he
told her, "in my cups." And he went on to ask her if she realized his wife was ruining him with her extravagance. "I send
her ten dollars every week of my unhappy life, and I don't
really have to. She threatens to jail me if I don't, but she can't
do it. God, let her try it after the way she treated me! She's no
right to alimony and she knows it. She keeps on saying she's
got to have it for the baby and I keep on sending it because I
can't bear to see anybody suffer. So I'm way behind on the
piano and the victrola, both—"

"Well, this is a pretty rug, anyhow," she said.

Bill stared at it and blew his nose. "I got it at Ricci's for ninety-five dollars," he said. "Ricci told me it once belonged to Marie Dressler, and cost fifteen hundred dollars, but there's a burnt place on it, under the divan. Can you beat that?"

"No," she said. She was thinking about her empty purse and that she could not possibly expect a check for her latest review for another three days, and her arrangement with the basement restaurant could not last much longer if she did not pay something on account. "It's no time to speak of it," she said, "but I've been hoping you would have by now that fifty dollars you promised for my scene in the third act. Even if it doesn't play. You were to pay me for the work anyhow out of your advance."

"Weeping Jesus," said Bill, "you, too?" He gave a loud sob, or hiccough, in his moist handkerchief. "Your stuff was no better than mine, after all. Think of that."

"But you got something for it," she said. "Seven hundred dollars."

Bill said, "Do me a favor, will you? Have another drink and forget about it. I can't, you know I can't, I would if I could, but you know the fix I'm in."

"Let it go, then," she found herself saying almost in spite of herself. She had meant to be quite firm about it. They drank again without speaking, and she went to her apartment on the floor above.

There, she now remembered distinctly, she had taken the letter out of the purse before she spread the purse out to dry.

She had sat down and read the letter over again: but there were phrases that insisted on being read many times, they had a life of their own separate from the others, and when she tried to read past and around them, they moved with the movement of her eyes, and she could not escape them . . . "thinking about you more than I mean to . . . yes, I even talk about you . . . why were you so anxious to destroy . . . even if I could see you now I would not . . . not worth all this abominable . . . the end . . ."

Carefully she tore the letter into narrow strips and touched a lighted match to them in the coal grate.

Early the next morning she was in the bathtub when the janitress knocked and then came in, calling out that she wished to examine the radiators before she started the furnace going for the winter. After moving about the room for a few minutes, the janitress went out, closing the door very sharply.

She came out of the bathroom to get a cigarette from the package in the purse. The purse was gone. She dressed and made coffee, and sat by the window while she drank it. Certainly the janitress had taken the purse, and certainly it would be impossible to get it back without a great deal of ridiculous excitement. Then let it go. With this decision of her mind, there rose coincidentally in her blood a deep almost murderous anger. She set the cup carefully in the center of the table, and walked steadily downstairs, three long flights and a short hall and a steep short flight into the basement, where the janitress, her face streaked with coal dust, was shaking up the furnace. "Will you please give me back my purse? There isn't any money in it. It was a present, and I don't want to lose it."

The janitress turned without straightening up and peered at her with hot flickering eyes, a red light from the furnace reflected in them. "What do you mean, your purse?"

"The gold cloth purse you took from the wooden bench in my room," she said. "I must have it back."

"Before God I never laid eyes on your purse, and that's the holy truth," said the janitress.

"Oh, well then, keep it," she said, but in a very bitter voice; "keep it if you want it so much." And she walked away.

She remembered how she had never locked a door in her life, on some principle of rejection in her that made her uncomfortable in the ownership of things, and her paradoxical boast before the warnings of her friends, that she had never lost a penny by theft; and she had been pleased with the bleak humility of this concrete example designed to illustrate and justify a certain fixed, otherwise baseless and general faith which ordered the movements of her life without regard to her will in the matter.

In this moment she felt that she had been robbed of an enormous number of valuable things, whether material or intangible: things lost or broken by her own fault, things she had forgotten and left in houses when she moved: books borrowed from her and not returned, journeys she had planned and had not made, words she had waited to hear spoken to her and had not heard, and the words she had meant to answer with; bitter alternatives and intolerable substitutes worse than nothing, and yet inescapable: the long patient suffereing of dying friendships and the dark inexplicable death of love—all that she had had, and all that she had missed, were lost together, and were twice lost in this landslide of remembered losses.

The janitress was following her upstairs with the purse in her hand and the same deep red fire flickering in her eyes. The janitress thrust the purse towards her while they were still a half dozen steps apart, and said: "Don't never tell on me. I musta been crazy. I get crazy in the head sometimes, I swear I do. My son can tell you."

She took the purse after a moment, and the janitress went on: "I got a niece who is going on seventeen, and she's a nice girl and I thought I'd give it to her. She needs a pretty purse. I musta been crazy; I thought maybe you wouldn't mind, you leave things around and don't seem to notice much."

She said: "I missed this because it was a present to me from someone . . ."

The janitress said: "He'd get you another if you lost this one. My niece is young and needs pretty things, we oughta give the young ones a chance. She's got young men after her maybe will want to marry her. She ought have nice things. She needs them bad right now. You're a grown woman, you've had your chance, you ought to know how it is!"

She held the purse out to the janitress saying: "You don't know what you're talking about. Here, take it, I've changed my mind. I really don't want it."

The janitress looked up at her with hatred and said: "I don't want it either now. My niece is young and pretty, she don't need fixin' up to be pretty, she's young and pretty anyhow! I guess you need it worse than she does!"

"It wasn't really yours in the first place," she said, turning away. "You mustn't talk as if I had stolen it from you."

"It's not from me, it's from her you're stealing it," said the janitress, and went back downstairs.

She laid the purse on the table and sat down with the cup of chilled coffee, and thought: I was right not to be afraid of any thief but myself, who will end by leaving me nothing.

[1930]

# MAY I FEEL SAID HE?

## ee cummings

May i feel said he
(i'll squeal said she
just once said he)
it's fun said she

(may i touch said he
how much said she
a lot said he)
why not said she

(let's go said he
not too far said she
what's too far said he
where you are said she)

may i stay said he
(which way said she
like this said he
if you kiss said she

may i move said he
is it love said she)
if you're willing said he
(but you're killing said she

but it's life said he
but your wife said she
now said he)
ow said she

(tiptop said he
don't stop said she
oh no said he)
go slow said she

(cccome? said he
ummm said she)
you're divine! said he
(you are Mine said she)

[1935]

# THE LIAR

## Tobias Wolff

MY MOTHER READ EVERYTHING EXCEPT BOOKS.
Advertisements on buses, entire menus as we ate, billboards; if
it had no cover it interested her. So when she found a letter in
my drawer that was not addressed to her she read it. "What
difference does it make if James has nothing to hide?"—that
was her thought. She stuffed the letter in the drawer when she
finished it and walked from room to room in the big empty
house, talking to herself. She took the letter out and read it
again to get the facts straight. Then, without putting on her
coat or locking the door, she went down the steps and headed
for the church at the end of the street. No matter how angry
or confused Mother might be, she always went to four o'clock
Mass and now it was four o'clock.

It was a fine day, blue and cold and still, but Mother
walked as though into a strong wind, bent forward at the
waist with her feet hurrying behind in short busy steps. My
brother and sisters and I considered this walk of hers funny,
and smirked at one another when she crossed in front of us to
stir the fire or water a plant. We didn't let her catch us at it. It
would have puzzled Mother to think that there might be anything amusing about her. Her one concession to the fact of
humor was an insincere, startling laugh. Strangers often stared
at her.

While Mother waited for the priest, who was late, she
prayed. She prayed in a familiar, orderly, firm way: first for
her late husband, my father, then for her parents—also dead.
She said a quick prayer for my father's parents (just touching
base—she had disliked them) and finally for her children in

order of their ages, ending with me. Mother did not consider originality a virtue, and until my name came up her prayers were exactly the same as on any other day.

But when she came to me she spoke up boldly. "I thought he wasn't going to do it anymore. Murphy said he was cured. What am I supposed to do now?" There was reproach in her tone. Mother put great hope in her notion that I was cured. She regarded my cure as an answer to her prayers and by way of thanksgiving sent a lot of money to the Thomasite Indian Mission, money she had been saving for a trip to Rome. She felt cheated and she let her feelings be known. When the priest came in Mother slid back on the seat and followed the Mass with concentration. After Communion she began to worry again and went straight home without stopping to talk to Frances, the woman who always cornered Mother after Mass to tell about the awful things done to her by communists, devil-worshippers, and Rosicrucians. Frances watched her go with narrowed eyes.

Once in the house, Mother took the letter from my drawer and brought it into the kitchen. She held it over the stove with her fingernails, looking away so that she would not be drawn into it again, and set it on fire. When it began to burn her fingers, she dropped it in the sink and watched it blacken and flutter and close upon itself like a fist. Then she washed it down the drain and called Doctor Murphy.

The letter was to my friend Ralphy in Arizona. He used to live across the street from us but he had moved. Most of the letter was about a tour of Alcatraz we, the junior class, had taken. That was all right. What got Mother was the last paragraph, where I said that she had been coughing up blood and the doctors weren't sure what was wrong with her, but that we were hoping for the best.

This wasn't true. Mother took pride in her physical condition, considered herself a horse: "I'm a regular horse," she would reply when people asked about her health. For several years now I had been saying unpleasant things that weren't true, and this habit of mine irked Mother greatly, enough to persuade her to send me to Doctor Murphy, in whose office I was sitting when she burned the letter. Doctor Murphy was our family physician and had no training in psychoanalysis, but he took an interest in "things of the mind," as he put it. He had treated me for appendicitis and tonsilitis and Mother thought that he could put the truth into me as easily as he took things out of me, a hope Doctor Murphy did not share. He was basically interested in getting me to understand what I did, and lately he had been moving toward the conclusion that I understood what I did as well as I ever would.

Doctor Murphy listened to Mother's account of the letter and what she had done with it. He was curious about the wording I had used and became irritated when Mother told him she had burned it. "The point is," she said, "he was supposed to be cured and he's not."

"Margaret, I never said he was cured."

"You certainly did. Why else would I have sent over a thousand dollars to the Thomasite mission?"

"I said that he was responsible. That means that James knows what he's doing, not that he's going to stop doing it."

"I'm sure you said he was cured."

"Never. To say that someone is cured, you have to know what health is. With this kind of thing that's impossible. What do you mean by curing James, anyway?"

"You know."

"Tell me anyway."

"Getting him back to reality, what else?"

"Whose reality? Mine or yours?"

"Murphy, what are you talking about? James isn't crazy, he's a liar."

"Well, you have a point there."

"What am I going to do with him?"

"I don't think there's much you can do. Be patient."

"I've been patient."

"If I were you, Margaret, I wouldn't make too much of this. James doesn't steal, does he?"

"Of course not."

"Or beat people up or talk back."

"No."

"Then you have a lot to be thankful for."

"I don't think I can take any more of it. That business about leukemia last summer. And now this."

"Eventually he'll outgrow it, I think."

"Murphy, he's sixteen years old. What if he doesn't outgrow it? What if he just gets better at it?"

Finally Mother saw that she wasn't going to get any satisfaction from Doctor Murphy, who kept reminding her of her blessings. She said something cutting to him and he said something pompous back and she hung up. Doctor Murphy stared at the receiver. "Hello," he said, then replaced it on the cradle. He ran his hand over his head, a habit remaining from a time when he had hair. To show that he was a good sport, he often joked about his baldness, but I had the feeling that he regretted it deeply. Looking at me across the desk, he must have wished that he hadn't taken me on. Treating a friend's child was like investing a friend's money.

"I don't have to tell you who that was."

I nodded.

Doctor Murphy pushed his chair back and swiveled it around so he could look out the window behind him, which took up most of the wall. There were still a few sailboats out on the Bay, but they were all making for shore. A woolly gray fog had covered the bridge and was moving in fast. The water seemed calm from this far up, but when I looked closely I could see white flecks everywhere.

"I'm surprised at you," he said. "Leaving something like

that lying around for her to find. If you really have to do these things, you could at least be kind and do them discreetly. It's not easy for your mother, what with your father dead and all the others somewhere else."

"I know. I didn't mean for her to find it."

"Well." He tapped his pencil against his teeth. He was not convinced professionally, but personally he may have been. "I think you ought to go home now and straighten things out."

"I guess I'd better."

"Tell your mother I might stop by, either tonight or tomorrow. And James—don't underestimate her."

While my father was alive we usually went to Yosemite for three or four days during the summer. My mother would drive and Father would point out places of interest, meadows where boomtowns once stood, hanging trees, rivers that were said to flow upstream at certain times. Or he read to us; he had the grown-ups' idea that children love Dickens and Sir Walter Scott. The four of us sat in the back seat with our faces composed, attentive, while our hands and feet pushed, pinched, stomped, goosed, prodded, dug, and kicked.

One night a bear came into our camp just after dinner. Mother had made a tuna casserole and it must have smelled to him like something worth dying for. He came into the camp while we were sitting around the fire and stood swaying back and forth. My brother, Michael, saw him first and elbowed me, then my sisters saw him and screamed. Mother and Father had their backs to him but Mother must have guessed what it was because she immediately said: "Don't scream like that. You might frighten him and there's no telling what he'll do. We'll just sing and he'll go away."

We sang "Row Row Row Your Boat," but the bear stayed. He circled us several times, rearing up now and then on his hind legs to stick his nose into the air. By the light of the fire I could see his doglike face and watch the muscles roll under his loose skin like rocks in a sack. We sang harder as he circled us, coming closer and closer. "All right," said Mother, "enough's enough." She stood abruptly. The bear stopped moving and watched her. "Beat it," said Mother. The bear sat down and looked from side to side. "Beat it," she said again, and leaned over and picked up a rock.

"Margaret, don't," said my father.

She threw the rock hard and hit the bear in the stomach. Even in the dim light I could see the dust rising from his fur. He grunted and stood to his full height. "See that?" Mother shouted. "He's filthy. Filthy!" One of my sisters giggled. Mother picked up another rock. "Please, Margaret," said my father. Just then the bear turned and shambled way. Mother pitched the rock after him. For the rest of the night he loitered around the camp until he found the tree where we had hung our food. He ate it all. The next day we drove back to the city. We could have bought more supplies in the valley, but Father wanted to go and would not give in to any argument. On the way home he tried to jolly everyone up by making jokes, but Michael and my sisters ignored him and looked stonily out the windows.

Things were never easy between my mother and me, but I didn't underestimate her. She underestimated me. When I was little she suspected me of delicacy, because I didn't like being thrown up into the air, and because when I saw her and the others working themselves up for a roughhouse, I found somewhere else to be. When they did drag me in I got hurt, a knee in the lip, a bent finger, a bloody nose, and this too Mother seemed to hold against me, as if I arranged my hurts to get out of playing.

Even things I did well got on her nerves. We all loved puns except Mother, who didn't get them, and next to my father I was the best in the family. My specialty was the Swifty— "'You can bring the prisoner down,' said Tom condescendingly." Father encouraged me to perform at dinner, which must have been a trial for outsiders. Mother wasn't sure what was going on, but she didn't like it.

She suspected me in other ways. I couldn't go to the movies without her examining my pockets to make sure I had enough money to pay for the ticket. When I went away to camp she tore my pack apart in front of all the boys who were waiting in the bus outside the house. I would rather have gone without my sleeping bag and a few changes of underwear, which I had forgotten, than be made such a fool of. Her distrust was the thing that made me forgetful.

And she thought I was coldhearted because of what happened the day my father died and later at his funeral. I didn't cry at my father's funeral, and showed signs of boredom during the eulogy, fiddling around with the hymnals. Mother put my hands into my lap and I left them there without moving them as though they were things I was holding for someone else. The effect was ironical and she resented it. We had a sort of reconciliation a few days later after I closed my eyes at school and refused to open them. When several teachers and then the principal failed to persuade me to look at them, or at some reward they claimed to be holding, I was handed over to the school nurse, who tried to pry the lids open and scratched one of them badly. My eye swelled up and I went rigid. The principal panicked and called Mother, who fetched me home. I wouldn't talk to her, or open my eyes, or bend, and they had to lay me on the back seat and when we reached the house Mother had to lift me up the steps one at a time. Then she put me on the couch and played the piano to me all afternoon. Finally I opened my eyes. We hugged each other and I wept. Mother did not really believe in my tears, but she was willing to accept them because I had staged them for her benefit.

My lying separated us too, and the fact that my promises not to lie anymore seemed to mean nothing to me. Often my lies came back to her in embarrassing ways, people stopping her in the street and saying how sorry they were to hear

that —————. No one in the neighborhood enjoyed embarrassing Mother, and these situations stopped occurring once
everybody got wise to me. There was no saving her from
strangers, though. The summer after Father died I visited my
uncle in Redding and when I got back I found to my surprise
that Mother had come to meet my bus. I tried to slip away
from the gentleman who had sat next to me but I couldn't
shake him. When he saw Mother embrace me he came up
and presented her with a card and told her to get in touch
with him if things got any worse. She gave him his card back
and told him to mind his own business. Later, on the way
home, she made me repeat what I had said to the man. She
shook her head. "It's not fair to people," she said, "telling
them things like that. It confuses them." It seemed to me that
Mother had confused the man, not I, but I didn't say so. I
agreed with her that I shouldn't say such things and promised
not to do it again, a promise I broke three hours later in conversation with a woman in the park.

It wasn't only the lies that disturbed Mother; it was their
morbidity. This was the real issue between us, as it had been
between her and my father. Mother did volunteer work at
Children's Hospital and St. Anthony's Dining Hall, collected
things for the St. Vincent de Paul Society. She was a lighter of
candles. My brother and sisters took after her in this way. My
father was a curser of the dark. And he loved to curse the
dark. He was never more alive than when he was indignant
about something. For this reason the most important act of
the day for him was the reading of the evening paper.

Ours was a terrible paper, indifferent to the city that
bought it, indifferent to medical discoveries—except for new
kinds of gases that made your hands fall off when you
sneezed—and indifferent to politics and art. Its business was
outrage, horror, gruesome coincidence. When my father sat
down in the living room with the paper, Mother stayed in the
kitchen and kept the children busy, all except me, because I

was quiet and could be trusted to amuse myself. I amused myself by watching my father.

He sat with his knees spread, leaning forward, his eyes only inches from the print. As he read he nodded to himself. Sometimes he swore and threw the paper down and paced the room, then picked it up and began again. Over a period of time he developed the habit of reading aloud to me. He always started with the society section, which he called the parasite page. This column began to take on the character of a comic strip or a serial, with the same people showing up from one day to the next, blinking in chiffon, awkwardly holding their drinks for the sake of Peninsula orphans, grinning under sunglasses on the deck of a ski hut in the Sierras. The skiers really got his goat, probably because he couldn't understand them. The activity itself was inconceivable to him. When my sisters went to Lake Tahoe one winter weekend with some friends and came back excited about the beauty of the place, Father calmed them right down. "Snow," he said, "is overrated."

Then the news, or what passed in the paper for news: bodies unearthed in Scotland, former Nazis winning elections, rare animals slaughtered, misers expiring naked in freezing houses upon mattresses stuffed with thousands, millions of dollars; marrying priests, divorcing actresses, high-rolling oilmen building fantastic mausoleums in honor of a favorite horse, cannibalism. Through all this my father waded with a fixed and weary smile.

Mother encouraged him to take up causes, to join groups, but he would not. He was uncomfortable with people outside the family. He and my mother rarely went out, and rarely had people in, except on feast days and national holidays. Their guests were always the same, Doctor Murphy and his wife and several others whom they had known since childhood. Most of these people never saw each other outside our house and they didn't have much fun together. Father discharged his obligations as host by teasing everyone about stupid things they had said or done in the past and forcing them to laugh at themselves.

Though Father did not drink, he insisted on mixing cocktails for the guests. He would not serve straight drinks such as rum and Coke, or even scotch on the rocks, only drinks of his own divising. He gave them lawyerly names such as "The Advocate," "The Hanging Judge," "The Ambulance Chaser," "The Mouthpiece," and described their concoction in detail. He told long, complicated stories in a near-whisper, making everyone lean in his direction, and repeated important lines; he also repeated the important lines in the stories my mother told, and corrected her when she got something wrong. When the guests came to the ends of their own stories he would point out the morals.

Doctor Murphy had several theories about Father, which he used to test on me in the course of our meetings. Doctor Murphy had by this time given up his glasses for contact lenses, and had lost weight in the course of fasts which he undertook regularly. Even with his baldness, he looked years younger than when he had come to the parties at our house. Certainly he did not look like my father's contemporary, which he was.

One of Doctor Murphy's theories was that Father had exhibited a classic trait of people who had been gifted children, by taking an undemanding position in an uninteresting firm. "He was afraid of finding his limits," Doctor Murphy told me. "As long as he kept stamping papers and making out wills, he could go on believing that he didn't *have* limits." Doctor Murphy's fascination with Father made me uneasy, and I felt traitorous listening to him. While he lived, my father would never have submitted to analysis; it seemed a betrayal to put him on the couch now that he was dead.

I did enjoy Doctor Murphy's recollections of Father when they were both in the Boy Scouts. Their troop had been on a long hike and Father had fallen behind. Doctor Murphy and the others decided to ambush him as he came down the trail.

They hid in the woods on each side and waited. But when Father walked into the trap none of them moved or made a sound and he strolled on without even knowing they were there. "He had the sweetest look on his face," said Doctor Murphy, "listening to the birds, smelling the flowers, just like Ferdinand the Bull." He also told me that my father's drinks tasted like medicine.

While I rode my bicycle from Doctor Murphy's office, Mother fretted. She felt terribly alone but she didn't call anyone because she also felt like a failure. My lying had that effect on her. She took it personally. At such times she did not think of my sisters, one happily married, the other doing brilliantly at Fordham. She did not think of my brother, Michael, who had given up college to work with runaway children in Los Angeles. She thought of me. She thought that she had made a mess of her family.

Actually she managed the family well. While my father was dying upstairs she pulled us together. She made lists of chores and gave each of us a fair allowance. Bedtimes were adjusted and she stuck by them. She set regular hours for homework. Each child was made responsible for the next eldest; and I was given a dog. She told us frequently, predictably, that she loved us. At dinner we were each expected to contribute something, and after dinner she played the piano and tried to teach us to sing in harmony, which I could not do. Mother, who was an admirer of the Trapp family, considered this a character defect.

Our life together was more orderly, healthy, while Father was dying that it had been before. He had set us rules to follow, not much different from the ones Mother gave us after he got sick, but he had administered them in a fickle way. Though we were supposed to get an allowance, we always had to ask him for it, and then he would give us too much because he enjoyed seeming magnanimous. Sometimes he punished us for no reason, because he was in a bad mood. He was likely to decide, as one of my sisters was going out to a dance, that she had better stay home and do something to improve herself. Or he would sweep us all up on a Wednesday night and take us ice-skating.

He changed after he learned about the cancer, and became more calm as the disease spread. He relaxed his teasing way with us, and from time to time it was possible to have a conversation with him which was not about the last thing that had made him angry. He stopped reading the paper and spent time at the window.

He and I became close. He taught me to play poker and sometimes helped me with my homework. But it wasn't his illness that drew us together. The reserve between us had begun to break down after the incident with the bear, during the drive home. Michael and my sisters were furious with him for making us leave early and wouldn't talk to him or look at him. He joked: though it had been a grisly experience we should grin and bear it, and so on. His joking seemed perverse to the others, but not to me. I had seen how terrified he was when the bear came into the camp. He had held himself so still that he had begun to tremble. When Mother started pitching rocks, I thought he was going to bolt, really. I understood—I had been frightened too. The others took it as a lark after they got used to having the bear around, but for me and Father it got worse through the night. I was glad to be out of there, grateful to Father for getting me out. I saw that his jokes were the way he held himself together. So I reached out to him with a joke: " 'There's a bear outside,' said Tom intently." The others turned cold looks on me. They thought I was sucking up. But Father smiled.

When I thought of other boys being close to their fathers, I thought of them hunting together, tossing a ball back and forth, making birdhouses in the basement, and having long talks about girls, war, careers. Maybe the reason it took us so long to get close was that I had this idea. It kept getting in the way of what we really had, which was a shared fear.

Anyway, we never had long talks, and when we were alone we didn't joke much. That was our way of keeping in touch when others were around. We played cards, seriously, to win. Toward the end he slept most of the time and I watched him. From below, sometimes, faintly, I heard Mother playing the piano. Occasionally he nodded off in his chair while I was reading to him; his bathrobe would fall open then, and I would see the long new scar on his stomach, red as blood against his white skin. His ribs all showed and his legs were like cables.

I once read in a biography of a great man that he "died well." I assume the writer meant that he kept his pain to himself, did not set off false alarms, and did not inconvenience too much those who were to stay behind. My father died well. His irritability gave way to something else, something like serenity. In the last days he went tender. It was as though he had been rehearsing the scene, as though the anger of his life had been a kind of stage fright. He managed his audience—us—with an old trouper's sense of when to clown and when to stand on his dignity. We were all moved, and admired his courage, as he intended we should. He died downstairs in a shaft of late afternoon sunlight on New Year's Day, while I was reading to him. I was alone in the house and didn't know what to do. His body did not frighten me but immediately and sharply I missed my father. It seemed wrong to leave him sitting up and I tried to carry him upstairs to the bedroom but it was too hard, alone. So I called up my friend Ralphy across the street. When he came over and saw what I wanted him for, he started crying, but I made him help me anyway. A couple of hours later Mother got home and when I told her that Father was dead she ran upstairs, calling his name. A few minutes later she came back down. "Thank God," she said, "at least he died in bed." This seemed important to her and I didn't tell her otherwise. But that night Ralphy's parents called. They were, they said, shocked at what I had done, and so was Mother when she heard the story, shocked and furious. Why? Because I had not told her the truth? Or because she had learned the truth, and could not go on believing that Father had died in bed? I really don't know.

"Mother," I said, coming into the living room, "I'm sorry about the letter. I really am."

She was arranging wood in the fireplace and did not look at me or speak for a moment. Finally she finished, straightened up and brushed her hands. She stepped back and looked at the fire she had laid. "That's all right," she said. "Not bad for a consumptive."

"Mother, I'm sorry."

"Sorry? Sorry you wrote it or sorry I found it?"

"I wasn't going to mail it. It was a sort of joke."

"Ha ha." She took up the whisk broom and swept bits of bark into the fireplace, then closed the drapes and settled on the couch. "Sit down," she said. She crossed her legs. "Listen, do I give you advice all the time?"

"Yes."

"I do?"

I nodded.

"Well, that doesn't make any difference, I'm supposed to. I'm your mother. I'm going to give you some more advice, for your own good. You don't have to make all these thing up, James. They'll happen anyway." She picked at the hem of her skirt. "Do you understand what I'm saying?"

"I think so."

"You're cheating yourself, that's what I'm trying to tell you. When you get to be my age, you won't know anything at all about life. All you'll know is what you've made up."

I thought about that. It seemed logical.

She went on. "I think maybe you need to get out of yourself more. Think more about other people."

The doorbell rang.

"Go see who it is," said Mother. "We'll talk about this later."

It was Doctor Murphy. He and Mother made their apologies and she insisted that he stay for dinner. I went to the kitchen to fetch ice for their drinks, and when I returned they were talking about me. I sat on the sofa and listened. Doctor Murphy was telling Mother not to worry. "James is a good boy," he said. "I've been thinking about my oldest, Terry. He's not really dishonest, you know, but he's not really honest either. I can't seem to reach him. At least James isn't furtive."

"No," said Mother, "he's never been furtive."

Doctor Murphy clasped his hands between his knees and stared at them. "Well, that's Terry. Furtive."

Before we sat down to dinner Mother said grace; Doctor Murphy bowed his head and closed his eyes and crossed himself at the end, though he had lost his faith in college. When he told me that during one of our meetings, in just those words, I had the picture of a raincoat hanging by itself outside a dining hall. He drank a good deal of wine and persistently turned the conversation to the subject of his relationship with Terry. He admitted that he had come to dislike the boy. Then he mentioned several patients of his by name, some of them known to Mother and me, and said that he disliked them, too. He used the word "dislike" with relish, like someone on a diet permitting himself a single potato chip. "I don't know what I've done wrong," he said abruptly, and with reference to no particular thing. "Then again maybe I haven't done anything wrong. I don't know what to think anymore. Nobody does."

"I know what to think," said Mother.

"So does the solipsist. How can you prove to a solipsist that he's not creating the rest of us?"

This was one of Doctor Murphy's favorite riddles, and almost any pretext was sufficient for him to trot it out. He was a child with a card trick.

"Send him to bed without dinner," said Mother. "Let him create that."

Doctor Murphy suddenly turned to me. "Why do you do it?" he asked. It was a pure question, it had no object beyond the satisfaction of his curiosity. Mother looked at me and there was the same curiosity in her face.

"I don't know," I said, and that was the truth.

Doctor Murphy nodded, not because he had anticipated my answer but because he accepted it. "Is it fun?"

"No, it's not fun. I can't explain."

"Why is it all so sad?" asked Mother. "Why all the diseases?"

"Maybe," said Doctor Murphy, "sad things are more interesting."

"Not to me," said Mother.

"Not to me, either," I said. "It just comes out that way."

After dinner Doctor Murphy asked Mother to play the piano. He particularly wanted to sing "Come Home, Abbie, the Light's on the Stair."

"That old thing," said Mother. She stood and folded her napkin deliberately and we followed her into the living room. Doctor Murphy stood behind her as she warmed up. Then they sang "Come Home, Abbie, the Light's on the Stair," and I watched him stare down at Mother intently, as if he were trying to remember something. Her own eyes were closed. After that they sang "Oh Magnum Mysterium." They sang it in parts and I regretted that I had no voice, it sounded so good.

"Come on, James," said Doctor Murphy as Mother played the last chords. "These old tunes not good enough for you?"

"He just can't sing," said Mother.

When Doctor Murphy left, Mother lit the fire and made more coffee. She slouched down in the big chair, sticking her legs straight out and moving her feet back and forth.

"That was fun," she said.

"Did you and Father ever do things like that?"

"A few times, when we were first going out. I don't think he really enjoyed it. He was like you."

I wondered if Mother and Father had had a good marriage. He admired her and liked to look at her; every night at dinner he had us move the candlesticks slightly to right and left of center so he could see her down the length of the table. And every evening when she set the table she put them in the center again. She didn't seem to miss him very much. But I wouldn't really have known if she did, and anyway I didn't miss him all that much myself, not the way I had. I thought about other things now, a lot of the time.

"James?"

I waited.

"I've been thinking that you might like to go down and stay with Michael for a couple of weeks or so."

"What about school?"

"I'll talk to Father McSorley. He won't mind. Maybe this problem will take care of itself if you start thinking about other people."

"I do."

"I mean helping them, like Michael does. You don't have to go if you don't want to."

"It's fine with me. Really. I'd like to see Michael."

"I'm not trying to get rid of you."

"I know."

Mother stretched, then tucked her feet under her. She sipped noisily at her coffee. "What did the word mean that Murphy used? You know the one?"

I thought. "Paranoid? That's where somebody thinks everyone is out to get him. Like that woman who always grabs you after Mass—Frances."

"Not paranoid. Everyone knows what that means. *Sol*—something."

"Oh. Solipsist. A solipsist is someone who thinks he creates everything around him."

Mother nodded and blew on her coffee, then put it down without drinking from it. "I'd rather be paranoid. Do you really think Frances is?"

"Of course. No question about it."

"I mean really *sick?*"

"That's what paranoid *is*, is being sick. What do you think, Mother?"

"What are you so angry about?"

"I'm not angry." I lowered my voice. "I'm not angry. But you don't believe those stories of hers, do you?"

"Well, no, not exactly. I don't think she knows what she's saying, she just wants someone to listen. She probably lives all by herself in some little room. So she's paranoid. Think of that. And I had no idea. James, we should pray for her. Will you remember to do that?"

I nodded. I thought of Mother singing "O Magnum Mysterium," saying grace, praying with easy confidence, and it came to me that her imagination was superior to mine. She could imagine things as coming together, not falling apart. She looked at me and I shrank; I knew exactly what she was going to say. "Son," she said, "do you know how much I love you?"

The next afternoon I took the bus to Los Angeles. I looked forward to the trip, to the monotony of the road and the empty fields by the roadside. Mother walked with me down the long concourse. The station was crowded and oppressive. "Are you sure this is the right bus?" she asked at the loading platform.

"Yes."

"It looks so old."

"Mother—"

"All right." She pulled me against her and kissed me, then held me an extra second to show that her embrace was sincere, not just like everyone else's, never having realized that everyone else does the same thing. I boarded the bus and we waved at each other until it became embarrassing. Then Mother began checking through her handbag for something. When she had finished I stood and adjusted the luggage over my seat. I sat and we smiled at each other, waved when the driver gunned the engine, shrugged when he got up suddenly to count the passengers, waved again when he resumed his seat. As the bus pulled out my mother and I were looking at each other with plain relief.

I had boarded the wrong bus. This one was bound for Los Angeles but not by the express route. We stopped in San Mateo, Palo Alto, San Jose, Castroville. When we left Castroville it began to rain, hard; my window would not close all the way, and a thin stream of water ran down the wall onto my seat. To keep dry I had to stay away from the wall and lean forward. The rain fell harder. The engine of the bus sounded as though it were coming apart.

In Salinas the man sleeping beside me jumped up but before I had a chance to change seats his place was taken by an enormous woman in a print dress, carrying a shopping bag. She took possession of her seat and spilled over onto half of mine, backing me up to the wall. "That's a storm," she said loudly, then turned and looked at me. "Hungry?" Without waiting for an answer she dipped into her bag and pulled out a piece of chicken and thrust it at me. "Hey, by God," she hooted, "look at him go to town on that drumstick!" A few people turned and smiled. I smiled back around the bone and kept at it. I finished that piece and she handed me another, and then another. Then she started handing out chicken to the people in the seats near us.

Outside of San Luis Obispo the noise from the engine grew suddenly louder and just as suddenly there was no noise at all. The driver pulled off to the side of the road and got out, then got on again dripping wet. A few moments later he

announced that the bus had broken down and that they were
sending another to pick us up. Someone asked how long that
might take and the driver said he had no idea. "Keep your
pants on!" shouted the woman next to me. "Anybody in a
hurry to get to L.A. ought to have his head examined."

The wind was blowing hard around the bus, driving sheets
of rain against the windows on both sides. The bus swayed
gently. Outside the light was brown and thick. The woman
next to me pumped all the people around us for their itiner-
aries and said whether or not she had ever been where they
were from or where they were going. "How about you?" She
slapped my knee. "Parents own a chicken ranch? I hope so!"
She laughed. I told her I was from San Francisco. "San
Francico, that's where my husband was stationed." She asked
me what I did there and I told her I worked with refugees
from Tibet.

"Is that right? What do you do with a bunch of Tibetans?"

"Seems like there's plenty of other places they could've
gone," said a man in front of us. "Coming across the border
like that. We don't go there."

"What do you do with a bunch of Tibetans?" the woman
repeated.

"Try to find them jobs, locate housing, listen to their prob-
lems."

"You understand that kind of talk?"

"Yes."

"Speak it?"

"Pretty well. I was born and raised in Tibet. My parents
were missionaries over there."

Everyone waited.

"They were killed when the communists took over." The
big woman patted my arm. "It's all right," I said.

"Why don't you say some of that Tibetan?"

"What would you like to hear?"

"Say 'The cow jumped over the moon'." She watched me,

smiling, and when I finished she looked at the others and shook her head. "That was pretty. Like music. Say some more."

"What?"

"Anything."

They bent toward me. The window suddenly went blind with rain. The bus driver had fallen asleep and was snoring softly to the swaying of the bus. Outside the muddy light flickered to pale yellow, and far off there was thunder. The woman next to me leaned back and closed her eyes and then so did the others as I sang to them in what was surely an ancient and holy tongue.

[1980]

# CHEAT STREET

## Cynthia Heimel

LET'S-CALL-HER-MARGARET COULDN'T SEE OUT OF THE TAXI because she was swoonily slumped against let's-call-him-Max, her head nestled into his chest as he crooned a George Jones tune into her hair.

"No, no," Margaret murmured, "this is unfair, this is cruel and unusual, this is way below the belt. Do not sing George Jones to me, I am a good girl."

"Margaret?"

"What?"

"Can we go out? Can we see each other?"

"Yes."

"You mean it?"

Margaret sat up and put her fingers into her hair so that her curls stood straight out. "Hello, I am Glenn Close," she said.

Max, to give him credit, burst out laughing.

And thus yet another woman decided to fuck a married man.

Infidelity is such a pretty word, so light and delicate. Whereas the act itself is dark and thick with guilt, betrayal, confusion, pain, and (okay) sometimes enormous pleasure.

I know Margaret very well, but it didn't help.

"Nothing you can say will make any difference," she said. "I already know everything. I know this will end at least in tears, and possibly in agony. I know that I am being a cliché and will soon begin to hate myself and think of myself as sordid and pathetic. I know that I might soon start entertaining fruitless fantasies of him leaving his wife and us living happily ever after, and the absurdity of thinking a man who cheats on one wife will not cheat on another. I know that we are playing with a stacked deck, that he has all the aces and I have no power, that I'll never be able to pick up the phone and just call him, even if my fusebox blows up at three A.M., that he can never be there for me. I know that I am indulging in a profoundly anti-feminist act and will probably go to hell. I know I am violating the fifth commandment and that I am immoral. And I know, God help me, that I could fall in love, and that then I will really be fucked."

"But you do realize," I said, "that by filling your life and dreams with this man, you're not leaving any room for a nice, decent, single guy who will bring you flowers and propose marriage?"

"Of course," she snapped. "What am I, dumb? Don't I have a shrink? Listen, this is not a pattern of mine. I don't have a string of married men in my past." Her face was red with feeling. "I have been waiting around for that mythical single man for three years! Nobody's even kissed me in a year! And then out of nowhere this amazing guy comes, and I am struck by a lighning bolt of lust. What would *you* do?"

"Jesus, you really are fucked," I said.

These times do not well accommodate infidelity. Those loopholes that were created in the '60s and '70s have been pulled tighter than Jesse Helms' sphincter. We no longer sanction open marriages or wife-swapping. We don't pretend anymore to be not jealous. We don't casually turn the other way while our mates "find some space." The sexual revolution is over, the days of randy experimentation dead.

Because there is *that disease*. We are understandably afraid to die. But even if there weren't *that disease*, we are immersed in the neo-fifties, a time of conservatism and blind patriotism, a time of born-again Christians and TV preachers and *Fatal Attraction*, of the reglorification of the nuclear family. If *Anna*

*Karenina* were written now, it would rocket to the top of the best-seller list.

But God or whatever is was that created the species has screwed us. We do not mate for life. Instead we have this overpowering sex drive. A crafty, irresponsible monster of a sex drive that rides roughshod over rules and morals and righteousness. A sex drive that makes fools of us all. So we can buy white wedding dresses and sharp tuxedos and order engraved matchbooks and promise in front of the entire world that we will, goddammit, be faithful for the rest of our lives, no kidding, and still some small, frightened part of our brains will be keening, "Well, anyway, I'll really try!"

No matter what our brains say, our bodies will do anything, anything, to get laid. It's bigger than all of us.

The more we try to deny the sex drive, to pretend it isn't there, the worse we will be destroyed. Witness (and laugh at) poor Jim Bakker, wretched Jimmy Swaggart. They tried like hell to put the lid on.

So who amongst us will cast the first stone at Margaret?

"I will," she says. "I will cast the first stone at myself. I am such an asshole. Why am I doing this? Women don't do this. Do they?"

"Of course we do," I said, "all the time. The most we can ever do to stop ourselves is to really, I mean really, try to be faithful, try not to go after another woman's man. To never do it lightly, or casually, or to get back at someone, or because we're bored or depressed or feeling fat. Because infidelity is serious shit. It deserves respect and fear."

"Did you hear about Beth?" she asked. "Fifteen years married to the same guy, suddenly she goes cold, can't sleep with him anymore, and she runs away with a sexy young penniless musician, and now instead of being an art patron she's waiting tables at a coffee shop?"

"Just goes to show you the lengths we will go to to get good sex," I said. "Meanwhile her husband, I happen to know, was having at least three affairs a year."

"*How* do you know?"

"Never you mind, missy. I'm just pointing out that even in this area, women are different."

[1988]

# THE MALTESE FALCON

## Dashiell Hammett

MISS WONDERLY, IN A BELTED GREEN CRÊPE SILK DRESS, opened the door of apartment 1001 at the Coronet. Her face was flushed. Her dark red hair, parted on the left side, swept back in loose waves over her right temple, was somewhat tousled.

Spade took off his hat and said: "Good morning."

His smile brought a fainter smile to her face. Her eyes, of blue that was almost violet, did not lose their troubled look. She lowered her head and said in a hushed, timid voice: "Come in, Mr. Spade."

She led him past open kitchen-, bathroom-, and bedroom-doors into a cream and red living-room, apologizing for its confusion: "Everything is upside-down. I haven't even finished unpacking."

She laid his hat on a table and sat down on a walnut settee. He sat on a brocaded oval-backed chair facing her.

She looked at her fingers, working them together, and said: "Mr. Spade, I've a terrible, terrible confession to make."

Spade smiled a polite smile, which she did not lift her eyes to see, and said nothing.

"That—that story I told you yesterday was all—a story," she stammered, and looked up at him now with miserable frightened eyes.

"Oh, that," Spade said lightly. "We didn't exactly believe your story."

"Then—?" Perplexity was added to the misery and fright in her eyes.

"We believed your two hundred dollars."

"You mean——?" She seemed to not know what he meant.

"I mean that you paid us more than if you'd been telling the truth," he explained blandly, "and enough more to make it all right."

Her eyes suddenly lighted up. She lifted herself a few inches from the settee, settled down again, smoothed her skirt, leaned forward, and spoke eagerly: "And even now you'd be willing to——?"

Spade stopped her with a palm-up motion of one hand. The upper part of his face frowned. The lower part smiled. "That depends," he said. "The hell of it is, Miss——Is your name Wonderly or Leblanc?"

She blushed and murmured: "It's really O'Shaughnessy—— Brigid O'Shaughnessy."

"The hell of it is, Miss O'Shaughnessy, that a couple of murders"——she winced——"coming together like this get everybody stirred up, make the police think they can go the limit, make everybody hard to handle and expensive. It's not——"

He stopped talking because she had stopped listening and was waiting for him to finish.

"Mr. Spade, tell me the truth." Her voice quivered on the verge of hysteria. Her face had become haggard around desperate eyes. "Am I to blame for——for last night?"

Spade shook his head. "Not unless there are things I don't know about," he said. "You warned us that Thursby was dangerous. Of course you lied to us about your sister and all, but that doesn't count: we didn't believe you." He shrugged his sloping shoulders. "I wouldn't say it was your fault."

She said, "Thank you," very softly, and then moved her head from side to side. "But I'll always blame myself." She put a hand to her throat. "Mr. Archer was so——so alive yesterday afternoon, so solid and hearty and——"

"Stop it," Spade commanded. "He knew what he was doing. They're the chances we take."

"Was——was he married?"

"Yes, with ten thousand insurance, no children, and a wife who didn't like him."

"Oh, please don't!" she whispered.

Spade shrugged again. "That's the way it was." He glanced at his watch and moved from his chair to the settee beside her. "There's no time for worrying about that now." His voice was pleasant but firm. "Out there a flock of policemen and assistant district attorneys and reporters are running around with their noses to the ground. What do you want to do?"

"I want you to save me from—from it all," she replied in a thin tremulous voice. She put a timid hand on his sleeve. "Mr. Spade, do they know about me?"

"Not yet. I wanted to see you first."

"What—what would they think if they knew about the way I came to you—with those lies?"

"It would make them suspicious. That's why I've been stalling them till I could see you. I thought maybe we wouldn't have to let them know all of it. We ought to be able to fake a story that will rock them to sleep, if necessary."

"You don't think I had anything to do with the—the murders—do you?"

Spade grinned at her and said: "I forgot to ask you that. Did you?"

"No."

"That's good. Now what are we going to tell the police?"

She squirmed on her end of the settee and her eyes wavered between heavy lashes, as if trying and failing to free their gaze from his. She seemed smaller, and very young and oppressed.

"Must they know about me at all?" she asked. "I think I'd rather die than that, Mr. Spade. I can't explain now, but can't you somehow manage so that you can shield me from them, so I won't have to answer their questions? I don't think I could stand being questioned now. I think I would rather die. Can't you, Mr. Spade?"

"Maybe," he said, "but I'll have to know what it's all about."

She went down on her knees at his knees. She held her face up to him. Her face was wan, taut, and fearful over tight-clasped hands.

"I haven't lived a good life," she cried. "I've been bad—worse than you could know—but I'm not all bad. Look at me, Mr. Spade. You know I'm not all bad, don't you? You can see that, can't you? Then can't you trust me a little? Oh, I'm so alone and afraid, and I've got nobody to help me if you won't help me. I know I've no right to ask you to trust me if I won't trust you. I do trust you, but I can't tell you. I can't tell you now. Later I will, when I can. I'm afraid, Mr. Spade. I'm afraid of trusting you. I don't mean that. I do trust you, but—I trusted Floyd and—I've nobody else, nobody else, Mr. Spade. You can help me. You've said you can help me. If I hadn't believed you could save me I would have run away today instead of sending for you. If I thought anybody else could save me would I be down on my knees like this? I know this isn't fair of me. But be generous, Mr. Spade, don't ask me to be fair. You're strong, you're resourceful, you're brave. You can spare me some of that strength and resourcefulness and courage, surely. Help me, Mr. Spade. Help me because I need help so badly, and because if you don't where will I find anyone who can, no matter how willing? Help me. I've no right to ask you to help me blindly, but I do ask you. Be generous, Mr. Spade. You can help me. Help me."

Spade, who had held his breath through much of this speech, now emptied his lungs with a long sighing exhalation between pursed lips and said: "You won't need much of anybody's help. You're good. You're very good. It's chiefly your eyes, I think, and that throb you get into your voice when you say things like 'Be generous, Mr. Spade.'"

She jumped up on her feet. Her face crimsoned painfully, but she held her head erect and she looked Spade straight in the eyes.

"I deserve that," she said. "I deserve it, but—oh!—I did want your help so much. I do want it, and need it, so much.

And the lie was in the way I said it, and not at all in what I said." She turned away, no longer holding herself erect. "It is my own fault that you can't believe me now."

Spade's face reddened and he looked down at the floor, muttering: "Now you are dangerous."

Brigid O'Shaughnessy went to the table and picked up his hat. She came back and stood in front of him holding the hat, not offering it to him, but holding it for him to take if he wished. Her face was white and thin.

Spade looked at his hat and asked: "What happened last night?"

"Floyd came to the hotel at nine o'clock, and we went out for a walk. I suggested that so Mr. Archer could see him. We stopped at a restaurant in Geary Street, I think it was, for supper and to dance, and came back to the hotel at about half-past twelve. Floyd left me at the door and I stood inside and watched Mr. Archer follow him down the street, on the other side."

"Down? You mean towards Market Street?"

"Yes."

"Do you know what they'd be doing in the neighborhood of Bush and Stockton, where Archer was shot?"

"Isn't that near where Floyd lived?"

"No. It would be nearly a dozen blocks out of his way if he was going from your hotel to his. Well, what did you do after they had gone?"

"I went to bed. And this morning when I went out for breakfast I saw the headlines in the papers and read about— you know. Then I went up to Union Square, where I had seen automobiles for hire, and got one and went to the hotel for my luggage. After I found my room had been searched yesterday I knew I would have to move, and I had found this place yesterday afternoon. So I came up here and then telephoned your office."

"Your room at the St. Mark was searched?" he asked.

"Yes, while I was at your office." She bit her lip. "I didn't mean to tell you that."

"That means I'm not supposed to question you about it?"

She nodded shyly.

He frowned.

She moved his hat a little in her hands.

He laughed impatiently and said: "Stop waving the hat in my face. Haven't I offered to do what I can?"

She smiled contritely, returned the hat to the table, and sat beside him on the settee again.

He said: "I've got nothing against trusting you blindly except that I won't be able to do you much good if I haven't some idea of what it's all about. For instance, I've got to have some sort of a line on your Floyd Thursby."

"I met him in the Orient." She spoke slowly, looking down at a pointed finger tracing eights on the settee between them. "We came here from Hongkong last week. He was— he had promised to help me. He took advantage of my help-lessness and dependence on him to betray me."

"Betray you how?"

She shook her head and said nothing.

Spade, frowning with impatience, asked: "Why did you want him shadowed?"

"I wanted to learn how far he had gone. He wouldn't even let me know where he was staying. I wanted to find out what he was doing, whom he was meeting, things like that."

"Did he kill Archer?"

She looked up at him, surprised. "Yes, certainly," she said.

"He had a Luger in a shoulder-holster. Archer wasn't shot with a Luger."

"He had a revolver in his overcoat-pocket," she said.

"You saw it?"

"Oh, I've seen it often. I know he always carries one there. I didn't see it last night, but I know he never wears an over-coat without it."

"Why all the guns?"

"He lived by them. There was a story in Hongkong that he

had come out there, to the Orient, as a bodyguard to a gambler who had had to leave the States, and that the gambler had since disappeared. They said Floyd knew about his disappearing. I don't know. I do know that he always went heavily armed and that he never went to sleep without covering the floor around his bed with crumpled newspaper so nobody could come silently into his room."

"You picked a nice sort of playmate."

"Only that sort could have helped me," she said simply, "if he had been loyal."

"Yes, if." Spade pinched his lower lip between finger and thumb and looked gloomily at her. The vertical creases over his nose deepened, drawing his brows together. "How bad a hole are you actually in?"

"As bad," she said, "as could be."

"Physical danger?"

"I'm not heroic. I don't think there's anything worse than death."

"Then it's that?"

"It's that as surely as we're sitting here"—she shivered—"unless you help me."

He took his fingers away from his mouth and ran them through his hair. "I'm not Christ," he said irritably. "I can't work miracles out of thin air." He looked at his watch. "The day's going and you're giving me nothing to work with. Who killed Thursby?"

She put a crumpled handkerchief to her mouth and said, "I don't know," through it.

"Your enemies or his?"

"I don't know. His, I hope, but I'm afraid—I don't know."

"How was he supposed to be helping you? Why did you bring him here from Hongkong?"

She looked at him with frightened eyes and shook her head in silence. Her face was haggard and pitifully stubborn.

Spade stood up, thrust his hands into the pockets of his

jacket, and scowled down at her. "This is hopeless," he said savagely. "I can't do anything for you. I don't know what you want done. I don't even know if you know what you want."

She hung her head and wept.

He made a growling animal noise in his throat and went to the table for his hat.

"You won't," she begged in a small choked voice, not looking up, "go to the police?"

"Go to them!" he exclaimed, his voice loud with rage. "They've been running me ragged since four o'clock this morning. I've made myself God knows how much trouble standing them off. For what? For some crazy notion that I could help you. I can't. I won't try." He put his hat on his head and pulled it down tight. "Go to them? All I've got to do is stand still and they'll be swarming all over me. Well, I'll tell them what I know and you'll have to take your chances."

She rose from the settee and held herself straight in front of him though her knees were trembling, and she held her white panic-stricken face up high though she couldn't hold the twitching muscles of mouth and chin still. She said: "You've been patient. You've tried to help me. It is hopeless, and useless, I suppose." She stretched out her right hand. "I thank you for what you have done. I—I'll have to take my chances."

Spade made the growling animal noise in his throat again and sat down on the settee. "How much money have you got?" he asked.

The question startled her. Then she pinched her lower lip between her teeth and answered reluctantly: "I've about five hundred dollars left."

"Give it to me."

She hesitated, looking timidly at him. He made angry gestures with mouth, eyebrows, hands, and shoulders. She went into her bedroom, returning almost immediately with a sheaf of paper money in one hand.

He took the money from her, counted it, and said: "There's only four hundred here."

"I had to keep some to live on," she explained meekly, putting a hand to her breast.

"Can't you get any more?"

"No."

"You must have something you can raise money on," he insisted.

"I've some rings, a little jewelry."

"You'll have to hock them," he said, and held out his hand. "The Remedial's the best place—Mission and Fifth."

She looked pleadingly at him. His yellow-grey eyes were hard and implacable. Slowly she put her hand inside the neck of her dress, brought out a slender roll of bills, and put them in his waiting hand.

He smoothed the bills out and counted them—four twenties, four tens, and a five. He returned two of the tens and the five to her. The others he put in his pocket. Then he stood up and said: "I'm going out and see what I can do for you. I'll be back as soon as I can with the best news I can manage. I'll ring four times—long, short, long, short—so you'll know it's me. You needn't go to the door with me. I can let myself out."

He left her standing in the center of the floor looking after him with dazed blue eyes.

[1929]

# FRANKIE AND JOHNNY

## Anonymous

FRANKIE AND JOHNNY WERE LOVERS
Said they were really in love;
Now, Frankie was true to her Johnny,
True as all the stars above;
He was her man, but he done her wrong.

Frankie and Johnny went walking,
Johnny had on a new suit;
That Frankie had bought with a "C-note"
'Cause it made him look so cute;
He was her man, but he done her wrong.

Johnny said, "I've got to leave now,
But I won't be very long;
Don't sit up and wait for me, honey,
Don't you worry while I'm gone;"
He was her man, but he done her wrong.

Frankie went down to the corner,
Stopped for a bottle of beer;
She said to the big fat bartender,
"Has my lovin' man been here?"
He was her man, but he done her wrong.

"Ain't gonna tell you no story,
Ain't gonna tell you no lie;
Your Johnny was here for a quick one
With a gal named Nelly Bly."
He was her man, but he done her wrong.

Anonymous

Frankie went home in a hurry,
She didn't go there for fun;
She opened a box on the dresser,
And got out her little gun.
He was her man, but he done her wrong.

Frankie went down to the corner,
Got in a cab, and she said,
"If I can locate that two-timer,
Won't be long before he's dead."
He was her man, but her done her wrong.

Frankie got out at Fourteenth Street
Looked in a window so high.
And there in the room was her Johnny
Makin' love to Nelly Bly.
He was her man, but he done her wrong.

Johnny saw Frankie a-comin,
Out the back way he did scoot,
But Frankie was quick on the trigger,
And the gun went "root-toot-toot."
He was her man, but he done her wrong.

They put her man in a coffin,
Brought out the rubber-tired hack,
And twelve men went out to the graveyard,
Just eleven came on back.
He was her man, but her done her wrong.

Sheriff arrested poor Frankie,
Put her in jail the same day:
He locked her up tight in that jail-house
And he threw the key away.
He was her man, but he done her wrong.

There is a point to this story,
Don't think it's only in fun;
Don't go on two-timin' your sweetie,
If the gal can use a gun.
He was her man, but he done her wrong.

[c. 1900]

# THE LIAR'S CLUB

## Mary Karr

DADDY HAD ONLY ONE LIARS' CLUB STORY THAT TOLD ME about his own momma's meanness, and that dealt with the blistering quality of her whippings, which were such that he bragged about having stood them. "The old lady would stripe my ass too. Don't think she wouldn't. Just as quick as Poppa would."

We're cleaning ducks—Daddy and I, and the other fellows. By nine this morning, we'd bagged our limit. I'm scooping the guts out of a little teal duck, and Daddy is pulling feathers from the huge slackened body of our only Canadian goose. With one swipe of his hand he clears a wide path in the feathers. "Momma was tough as a wood-hauler's ass," he says, and that's high praise. Back in the logging camp, wood haulers drove mule-drawn wagons of raw lumber. Since their butts rubbed up against unstripped pine all day, they became badges of toughness.

"How many eggs ya'll want?" Ben wants to know. Everybody says three. He slides a big slab of Crisco into the black skillet. We stopped here at Cooter's one-room cabin to clean ducks and eat breakfast. It's on the Chupique Bayou, just across the river in Louisiana.

"Not as big as a minute, my mother," Daddy says. "But mean as a snake if you ever lied to her."

Shug then says with a straight face that he can't imagine Daddy *ever* lying. He's quartering the ducks and wrapping the pieces in white freezer paper for us to divvy up when we're back in town.

Daddy tilts his head at Shug. "Last time she ever whupped on me was over lying. I had got big enough to figure I was too big to whup. Hell, my arms was that big around." He stares into the washtub full of duck carcass and feathers at his feet like it's some oracle his momma's ghost is about to rise out of.

When he's sure everybody's listening, he backs up to set the scene. "Had come a hurricane that August. Dumped umpteen-zillion gallons of water in the Neches River. High?" He glares at each one of us so we get the point. "Lord God, that river was high." The room sits quiet, the only noises the pop of eggs sliding in grease and Shug folding up the butcher paper. For a split second, the word "hurricane" sends roaring out of my own head at me a memory of the Orange Bridge during Hurricane Carla—how the railing had come rushing sideways at the car through the rain. I shake my head loose from that and get back to my teal ducks. It's sticky work.

"I remember that storm," Cooter says. He's got a little wire of excitement in his voice at the idea of actually being in on the story.

"Cooter, you was still shitting yellow back then," Ben says, "if you was drawing breath at all." He breaks the yolks with his spatula so the eggs fry up hard. To get eggs like this in a truck stop, you say to the lady, *Turn 'em over and step on 'em.*

"Well, I remember one like it," Cooter says.

"Hell, we all remember one like it," Shug says. He's about fed up with Cooter, who's been bossing him all weekend because he's colored. *Shug, get the outboard. Shug, you're shooting too soon. Goddammit, Shug, I was saving them biscuits for later.* Cooter is also just walking the edge of telling colored jokes. He uses *Polack* and *Aggie*, but everybody—Shug included—knows that if there wasn't a black man holding down a chair in this room they'd be nigger this and nigger that. Daddy says Cooter's just ignorant, never knew anybody colored before, so it's not his fault. But it seems mean how nobody ever says anything back directly. I mean, the guys do try to corral him a little and keep him from being overmuch an asshole. But nobody says flat out *You're just picking on Shug because he's colored*. It sometimes seems to me like we're not supposed to notice that Shug's colored, or that saying anything about it would be bad manners. That puzzles me because Shug's being colored strikes me as real obvious. And usually anybody's difference gets pounced on and picked at. This silence is a lie peculiar to a man's skin color, which makes it extra serious and extra puzzling.

Daddy's voice stops me wondering. "Anyways, Momma told me and my brother A.D. flat out not to go into that river. 'Stay out of that river, boys. They's boys drowned in that river.' And we said okay. But A.D. cut me a little look. And I knew we thinking the same thing.

"Me and old A.D. go squat outside the window and talk real loud so she'll hear us. Say we oughta go down the sawmill. See if Poppa needs any help. We take off down that woods road. But soon as we hit the fork where she can't see"—he forks his fingers like a road he's arriving at—"we peel off and go yonder a ways. The rest of them boys was gonna be down at the water. So that's where we want to be too. We got there and stripped on down and dove just as straight in that river as a pair of butter knives."

Daddy's done plucking the goose and hands me the prickly pink body to gut. He picks up a mallard. Its head is an iridescent green. When Ben was toting all the mallards up from the duck blind earlier this morning, all their green shiny heads came together in his big red hand like a bouquet of flowers. But for their black eyes staring out, you could almost forget they're dead.

"And this was your oldest brother you was with?" Cooter asks.

"It don't matter who it was, Cooter," Shug says. "Goddamn, you're the asking-est sonofabitch I ever met."

Cooter twists around on the chair and stares at Shug. Cooter maintains a birdlike way of twitching his head around that makes me think sometimes that he's about to go clucking off across the room pecking at the floorboards. "It matters if I feel like knowing," Cooter says.

Daddy draws back the mallard in his hand like it's a ball bat he's fixing to swing. "I swear to God, I'm gonna flail both your asses with this duck if you don't shut up," he says.

"He started it," Cooter says, then sinks back down in his shirt collar.

Ben says to let it go. He's over at the stove, pouring off the extra grease from the skillet into the lard pot.

Daddy takes a few swipes at the mallard to get everybody's eyes back on him before he starts up again. "That evening we head down through them woods back home, and here comes Momma. She'd got her apron pulled around and tucked in her skirt so the brush don't catch it. And she always wore a old blue-flowered bonnet." Daddy fans his hands behind his head to show the bonnet. "The sun was going down to the west, which was her right side. So that bonnet th'owed a shadow across't her face. Kept us from seeing her. But I could tell by how she was stomping through those weeds that she was mad. Plus she'd already cut herself a piss elum pole about as long as she was tall. Like she'd got it in her head already to whup us. I whisper over my shoulder to A.D. not to tell her we went in. Just to say we watched the other boys. And he says okay.

"Not a minute later she stops square on that path in front of me. 'J.P.,' she says, 'you go in that river?'

" 'No'm,' I says, 'we just watched them other boys.' And she says fine. Then she reaches that pole around behind me and taps A.D. on the shoulder. Just light enough to get his attention. 'A.D., did you go in that river?' And damned if he don't say, 'Yes'm. I went in, and he came in with me,' And I thinks to myself, you sorry sonofabitch."

I watch Ben draw a cake pan of biscuits out of the oven. He uses a pointy bottle opener to pop a triangular hole in a brand-new yellow can of sugarcane syrup. I like to poke a hole in a biscuit with my thumb, then fill it with that syrup so it gushes out the sides when you bite down. I figure on doing that, which fills the back of my mouth up with longing for the sweetness of it. I'm still holding that sweetness like a thirst when Daddy starts up.

"Lemme tell you fellas, my momma at that time wasn't no bigger than Mary Marlene here." He jerks his thumb at me so I can prove his mother's tininess. I ignore this by faking big-time interest in slitting open the fat belly of this goose. "Probably didn't weigh ninety pounds with boots on, my momma. Anyways, she took us out on the screened-in back porch—we slept out there in the summer. Started in on him with that pole and like to have killed him. Brought it down on his back in one narrow swatch, like she was trying to cut a groove through his flesh. I'd laugh like hell every time his eyes caught mine. I figured she was getting wore out on him. So's my turn wouldn't be as bad."

Shug says, "My daddy beat me and my brother thataways. Taking turns, so one watched the other."

"Now you're interrupting!" Cooter says, slapping the table. "Why don't nobody stop him interrupting?" The veins are standing out on Cooter's neck. Ben tells him to get the plates down and stop feeling sorry for hisself.

Daddy drops the mallard in the tub like he's all of a sudden exhausted by thinking again about that whipping. The whole burden of it seems to fall on him full force. His shoulders slump. The deep lines of his face get deeper. Then he gets an unfocused look at the middle distance like the beating's happening right in the room, and all he has to do is watch it and report back to the other guys. "That pole of hers cut the shirt right off my back in about four swipes." His head drops lower, as if under the weight of that pole, which is getting easier by the minute for me to imagine. "I've had grown men beat on me with tire irons and socks full of nickels and every conceivable kind of stick. But that old woman shrunk up like a pullet hen took that piss elum pole and flat set me on fire from my shoulders clear down past my ass. And every time she said a word, she brought that pole down. 'Don't—you—lie—to—me—Don't—you—run—from—me!' Hell, I broke loose from her a couple of times. And I run to the screen door. But the pine boards on that old sleeping porch was swole up from that rain. The door was swole. So I couldn't pull it flush all the way, couldn't get the latch unhooked. I'd just about get it wiggled tight in the frame, and then that pole would find my back again. You could her it come whistling through the air just a heartbeat before you felt it. And Momma behind it just hacking at me like I was a pine she was trying to knock over. I was scared to fall. Scared I wouldn't live to get vertical again. I promise you that. You think she was wore out on A.D.?" He squints at us, then picks up the mallard again and picks at a few of the quills like he's winding down. "Hell, she just warmed up on A.D."

"They hate that when you run," Ben says. He's sliding the last egg onto the platter. "My grandma was the same exact way. Running just dragged it out." Of course, I am famous for running in the middle of a spanking. It makes me proud that Daddy used to run too. I always figured only a dumbass would just stand still and take it. I have maneuvered my way over by the stove and am eye level now with the plate of biscuits, which have plumped up nice and brown on top. The slightest blink from Ben saying okay, and I will snatch the first one.

"I finally broke straight through the middle of that screen," Daddy says. "Left a outline of myself cut clean around the edges as a paper doll." Shug winks at me over the unlikeliness of this. He always keeps me posted as to the believability quotient of what Daddy's saying, even though I'm a kid, and a notorious pain in the ass as kids go.

Daddy sets down the duck again, and a smile stretches across his face, his eyes crinkle up, and his shoulders go square like the best part of the story just bubbled back up in him. "And old A.D. had hell to pay. Don't think he didn't."

"Wasn't Uncle A.D. a lot bigger than you, Daddy?" I am always trying to figure a way around my own skinniness. Uncle A.D. is a big oak tree of a man, white-headed and strong. In all the pictures of the Karr boys lined up, he stands close to Daddy and stares down his nose, like he's lording something over him.

"Don't make no difference, bigger," Daddy says. "Bigger's just one thing. They's a whole lot of other things than bigger, Pokey. Don't you forget it. Bigger's ass, was what I thought.

"I head out behind the shed," Daddy says, "and there's old A.D. hunkered down on the ground. 'Say, brother,' I says to him." Daddy's voice as he makes out talking to Uncle A.D. is smooth and sweet as melty butter. " 'I believe you made out pretty bad back there.' I tell him I got some burn salve may take that sting out. And A.D. he bends over. Starts picking at that shirt on his back where that fabric's stuck down in them sores. He's a-hissing between his teeth. Gets that old cotton blouse pulled up over his shoulder blades, then asks me does that look bad. And I say, 'Poor old you.' Course she cut the shirt slap off my back. 'Pull your shirt off your neck a little higher,' I says to him. 'I don't want to get this here salve on it. Piss Momma off any worse.' So he bends way over further. Gets bent double-like. His arms all hung up in them shirt-sleeves till he's stuck like a snake in a sock. That's when I grab hold to him. Pour that old turpentine horse liniment down in them sores. Was a deep, purple-black liniment Momma made from tar. I held him still and smeared it in with the flat of my hand. And him wrassling me to break loose."

Shug stops wrapping bird carcasses a second. He tilts his head at Daddy, then says that his momma cooked up some horse liniment back then out of a tar base. See, Shug's from up in the piney woods too. "Hers was tar and pine sap, I remember right. Maybe she put some lemon grass in it, one of them stingy herbs." Shug's momma knew Daddy's momma. They were both pretty good country doctors, and every now and then Shug and Daddy ride back toward their mothers into that place to get to something like this liniment, or some other doctoring recipe. The looks on their faces grow so vaguely soft that I feel tears start in back of my eyes. I am verging on lonesome myself for these women I never knew.

Daddy says that sounds like the exact stuff. He stands from the washtub of feathers and sidles over to the sink to wash up. He seems pleased. Shug's knowing the very liniment proves that the world Daddy's telling exists. But Shug's brow has grown a furrow like it bothers him. He claims to Daddy that you couldn't get that stuff off you, not out of a cut or something. And Daddy says that was the very idea, to scald Uncle A.D. down to the bone for tattling on him.

This sets me wondering. I hear about Daddy doing this kind of meanness, and I see guys shy away when he strolls over to a pool table, but he handles me like I'm something glass. Even his spankings are mild enough to seem symbolic. When I got up cold this morning before we set out for the bayou, he warmed my socks over the gas heater before I pulled them on. (Lecia was sleeping over at a friend's that morning, having outgrown Daddy somehow, having also gotten agile at worming her way into families quieter than ours.) My daddy buys me whatever I ask for and laughs at my jokes and tells me he loves me better than anybody about fifty times a day. I've seen him fight, but I've never seen this sneaky meanness he talks about at the Liars' Club. I look at him scrubbing the blood out from under his fingernails with a pale blue plastic brush and wonder about it. He's laughing like hell over what he did to A.D. Daddy pats his hands dry on a dish towel. "I left old A.D. squirming on the ground. Scrabbling to get away from hisself."

Ben upends the pan of biscuits, which fall out of the tin in a perfect steaming circle. They're crusty brown on the bottom. He nods at me to tear one loose, and I do. But I have to hot-potato it hand to hand to keep it from burning me. Finally, I drop it on the counter and cup my hands over it in a little igloo that I blow on. When I look up from that, I see that Ben also has a dark look on his face, like he can't get away from the meanness of this story fast enough either.

[1995]

# SOME CLOWNING THAT WASN'T IN THE ACT

## Groucho Marx

MANY YEARS AGO, WHEN WE WERE STILL IN THE SMALL TIME (and not doing particularly well), we were playing the college town of Williamstown. Appearing on the bill with us were two young, beautiful, untalented sisters who, for the purpose of this story, we will call the Delaney twins. If I were to use their real names the more elderly of my readers would remember them, for later in their careers they became rather notorious.

Despite the fact that they possessed a notable lack of talent, they were so pretty, youthful and shapely that no one seemed to care what they did on the stage. This being a college town, the audience was composed mostly of students who, like their contemporaries all over the world, were simply mad about young, beautiful girls.

The applause at the conclusion of their act was raucous, vociferous and insistent, and to restrain the students from rushing up on the stage and attacking them publicly, the girls hastily did their entire act over again.

After the ovation subsided, we appeared. We were fairly talented at the time, and by virtue of having more people in our group than any other number on the bill, we were the headliners. Apparently the audience wasn't impressed with our billing—or our act. Or perhaps they were still thinking of those two sexpots whose lovely shapes had transported them, even if only temporarily, into a heaven that is reserved for men under twenty-five. At any rate, to get this paragraph off the ground, we laid a large-sized egg. I have no way of knowing the precise temperature in the theatre during our performance that afternoon but, roughly, I would say it was about the same temperature as the water that flowed around the exterior of the *Nautilus* the day it sailed under the North Pole.

By the time we had finished, removed our make-up and dressed, the twins had left the theatre. Their dressing-room door was ajar and, as we walked past, we spotted some shapeless objects dangling on a hook. They looked suspiciously like symmetricals. In case you weren't a woman thirty years ago, I'll explain what symmetricals were. Let's say your legs and thighs were too thin and you were generally on the scrawny side. You simply encased the lower part of your carcass in this "stuffing," and over it you wore opera-length stockings. Though you might look like an underfed turkey in the shower, once you donned these pads all your basic imperfections disappeared and your shape rose and fell in all the places where your Creator had originally played you a dirty trick.

It embarrasses me to tell you what happened next. A confession of this kind should never be made publicly, but should only be revealed to your personal head-shrinker. Even though it happened more than thirty years ago, I'm still ashamed of my behavior. Posting Gummo (who was basically a peeping Tom) at the door as a lookout, I furtively stole into their dressing room, quickly lifted the symmetricals off the hook, took them to my hotel and gently laid them away in a dresser drawer.

That evening, when we returned to the theatre, there was a tremendous commotion going on backstage. We could hear the manager shouting that dreary, inevitable cry, "The show must go on!"—mingled with the sobs of the lovely twins, hysterically insisting that it was impossible for them to appear. The manager, puzzled, kept asking why. They finally broke down and told him about the lower "falsies," conceding that without them they were just two thin girls without much talent. They had looked everywhere, they added, but the foundation of their act had mysteriously disappeared.

In the midst of the tumult, I, hypocrite that I was, sauntered into the girls' dressing room and innocently inquired what all the shouting was about. They were too embarrassed to tell me. The manager, never one to let modesty come between him and the box office, yelled, "Some dirty bastard sneaked in here and stole the girls' shapes! And now, with a sold-out house full of students, they flatly refuse to go on!" (Knowing what I did, I found the word "flatly" rather amusing.)

"Well," I said, rather airily, "don't worry about the students. They'll see us."

"The hell with you and your brothers!" retorted the manager. "That audience out front wants to see these girls. They're not interested in your lousy act!" He looked frantically around the room. "Now where can those damned symmetricals be?"

At the word "symmetricals," I gallantly averted my gaze. The twins blushed to the roots of their hair, which I now noticed had recently been touched up. "Hmmm," I said, in my best Sherlock Holmes manner, "can't find 'em, eh? Well, you know this is a college town, and it's my guess that a couple of love-crazed students sneaked backstage between the matinee and evening performances and, just as a boyish prank, hooked the pads." As an afterthought, I asked, "Were they insured?"

With that, the two skinny young beauties burst into a new storm of tears, and the manager threw up his hands in defeat and stalked out.

Since the twins couldn't appear that evening, and the only other number was a dog act, we were a tremendous hit. I don't know about Gummo, but I slept badly that night. I kept thinking about those two poor, helpless, shapeless girls, with a substantial part of them reposing in my dresser drawer. It was a dirty trick, and I lay in bed wallowing in my own guilt. They were nice kids, I thought, and had they been a trifle fleshier I could have fallen in love with either one . . . or both.

By morning, my conscience had me down for the count. I put the symmetricals in my suitcase and, before breakfast, without consulting Gummo, took them back to the theatre. After making sure no one was around, I sneaked into the dressing room and hung their act back on the empty hook.

The girls appeared that evening. They were a huge success and, as usual, we flopped. But despite our inability to entertain the audience, I slept much better that night.

[1959]

# EIGHT MEN OUT

## John Sayles

383  EXT. STREET—NIGHT
*Buck is walking home alone. Scooter and Bucky wait for him on a stoop—*

SCOOTER
**Hey, Buck.**

BUCK
**Hey, fellas.**
*Buck sits down by them. He needs somebody to talk to—*

SCOOTER
**We seen you outside the court.**

BUCK
*(shakes his head)*
**Some circus, huh?**

SCOOTER
**Is it true what they're sayin' in there? About Joe and the others?**

BUCK
**Don't be too down on the guys. When you grow up, things get— *complicated.***

LITTLE BUCKY
**But you didn't do nothing wrong, didja Buck?**

John Sayles

BUCK
*(shrugs)*
**Guess I never grew up.**
*A silence as Buck thinks, troubled—*

BUCK
**You get out there and the stands are full and you hear
'em cheerin—like all the people in the world come to
see you—and inside of that there's the players and
they're yakkin it up and the pitcher throws and you
look for that pill and suddenly there's nothin else in the
ballpark but you and it. And sometimes—sometimes
when you're feelin right there's a groove there and your
bat just eases into it and meets that ball—when it meets
that ball and you can feel that ball just *give* and you
know it's going a long way and damn if you don't feel
like you're gonna live forever—**
*He is silent again. The kids watch, puzzled but fascinated by his
emotion—*

BUCK
**I couldn't give that up. Not for nothin.**

SCOOTER
**How you think they're gonna call it tomorrow?**

BUCK
*(defiant)*
**You look down to third base next year, you're gonna
see Buck Weaver, playin his butt off.**

SCOOTER
*(smiles)*
**Yeah.**

384 INT. COURTROOM — CLERK *(reading)*

CLERK
'**—have been accused of conspiracy to commit a confidence game, an offense which in this case carries a maximum penalty of five years in jail and a two thousand dollar fine. Does any one of you have a statement to make before the final verdict is read?'**

385 BUCK
*Jumps to his feet—*

BUCK
**I do your honor!**
*Swede and Chick roll their eyes.*

JUDGE *(off)*
**Very well, Mr Weaver.**

BUCK
**I'd like it put down in the record somewheres that I asked to be tried separately and was refused—**

386 LANDIS
*Watching impassively—*

BUCK *(off)*
**—that evidence of my play in the Series games was not admitted—**

387 COURTROOM

BUCK
**—and that I never got a chance to take the stand in my own behalf.**

JUDGE
**It will be so noted. Foreman, would you read the verdict?**

388 PLAYERS
*Waiting, tense—*

389 HUGH AND RING
*Exchanging a look. It could go either way—*

390 FOREMAN

FOREMAN
**Yes Your Honor.**
*(grins)*
**We find the defendants not guilty of all charges.**

391 COURTROOM
*Whooping, clapping, whistling. Fans mobbing the players—*

392 KID
*Smiles, with mixed emotions—*

393 HUGH AND RING

RING
**That wraps it up, sports fans.**

HUGH
**Gamblers eight, baseball nothing.**

394 COMISKEY AND AUSTRIAN
*The lawyer claps his disgruntled client on the back—*

AUSTRIAN
**You've got your ballclub back, Commy.**

COMMY
**I'll make them pay for this—**

395 PLAYERS
*Lefty and Joe are carried on the shoulders of the crowd. They lead us to Judge Landis, standing, watching, still taking notes—*

396 EXT. ITALIAN RESTAURANT — NIGHT
*A car full of celebrants cruises by with much HONKING and SHOUTING—*

397 INT. RESTAURANT
*The eight cleared players enter in high spirits. They see that the lawyers from both sides and most of the jurors are already there at a large table—*

CHICK
**Hey, small world, huh? Mind if we join youse?**

SHORT
**Why not? Push those tables over here—**

FOREMAN
**Make room for the Clean Sox!**
*As the players join them the lawyers and jury congratulate them, and all seems to be forgotten.*

AHEARN
**How you feelin Joe?**

JOE
**Like a million bucks.**

FOREMAN
**Attaboy!**

JOE
**I seen some lawyerin in my day but you people in Chicago got some lawyerin birds! Talk the buffalo right off the nickel if they put their minds to it—**
*A big laugh from the group—*

398 INT. LEGAL STUDY—JUDGE LANDIS—NEWS-MEN
*The Judge is reading a prepared statement to the gathered newsmen, including Ring and Hugh, in his dim-lit study—*

LANDIS
**'Regardless of the verdict of juries, no player who throws a ball game, no player who undertakes or promises to throw a game, no player who—'**

399 INT. RESTAURANT
*We CONTINUE to hear the Judge in VOICEOVER as we see the boys in SLOW MOTION, whooping it up over their ziti and meatballs. We PAN along, seeing each of the players—Hap balancing a meatball on his nose, Chick and Swede teasing Joe as McMullin arrives with drinks for them, Eddie and Lefty just laughing along, and Buck sitting a little to the side, forcing a laugh—*

LANDIS (VO, contd)
**'—sits in conference with a bunch of crooked players and gamblers where the ways and means of throwing a ball game are discussed and does not promptly tell his club about it—will ever play professional baseball again.'**

*We FREEZE the ballplayers in a joyous tableau,
then DISSOLVE TO:*

EXT. BASEBALL FIELD — DAY — SCOREBOARD
*A KID sits on scaffolding in front of a rickety scoreboard with wooden letters in his lap, waiting for the score to change. We hear players CHATTERING, a small crowd BUZZING, and over his shoulder the lettering tells us that WEEHAWKEN is facing JERSEY CITY today—*
KID'S POV FIELD
*A small wooden stadium, a semi-pro team in the field, a few men on base, and a hundred people scattered in the stands having a great time. We SUPERIMPOSE—*

**1925**

STANDS — FANS
*We PAN down a row of FANS, all men in their 30's or 40's except PAUL, an adolescent.*

RED
**Fella's playin kinda shallow in center, isn't he?**

BUD
**He's new.**

LES
**Damn if that doesn't look like him—**

PAUL
**Look like who?**

LES
**Naaah—couldn't be—**

RED
**He's gonna get burned, playin that close in—**

BATTER
*The BATTER, a kid in his late teens, whacks a long fly to center—*

CENTER FIELD
*The CENTERFIELDER, his back to us, runs to the fence and makes a great over-the-shoulder catch. As he turns to toss the ball back in we see that it is Joe Jackson—*

FANS
*Standing as the crowd reacts to the catch, ending the inning.*

RED
**How'd he get back there?**

BUD
**Who is that guy?**

CLOSE UP ON JOE
*Trotting to the infield. He looks peaceful and innocent moving on a ballfield again—*

LES *(off)*
**It is. It's him.**

PAUL
**It's who?**

FANS

BUD
**What's his name, the new guy?**

RED
**He don't look so new to me.**

PAUL
(looks at program)
**Says his name is Brown.**

LES
**A name is easy to change. It's *him*.**

PAUL
**Who's *him*?**

JOE
*Swinging a couple of bats as he gets ready to come to the plate—*

LES (off)
**It's Joe Jackson.**

FANS
*The older guys look at Les like he's screwy.*

RED
**What?**

BUD
**Get outa here—**

PAUL
**Who's Joe Jackson?**

LES
**Lookit how he's hitting—he's killin us out there—home run, two doubles—**

BUD
**These bushers make peanuts, Les. Jackson made a fortune on those games—**

LES
**It's him.**

RED
**You ever see him play?**

LES
**I saw pictures.**

RED
*(scornful)*
**Pictures.**

PAUL
**Who's Joe Jackson?**

BUCK *(off)*
**I saw him play.**

*We SHIFT to include the guy sitting next to Paul, a somber looking guy in a dark hat. It is Buck Weaver—*

RED
**Yeah? So what do you think?**

BUCK
*(shrugs)*
**He was the best.**

JOE
*Stepping into the batter's box—*

BUCK *(off)*
**Hit, run, throw—he was the best.**

PAUL *(off)*
**Who's Joe Jackson?**

FANS
*All eyes on Buck now—*

RED
**Is that him?**

*Buck looks out on the field, darkening—*
BUCK
**Nah. Those fellas are all gone now.**

PAUL
**What fellas?**

JOE
*Steps into a fastball—WHACK!*

OUTFIELDER
*Scurrying back as the ball sails over his head—*

FANS
*Up on their feet as the crowd ROARS—*

LES
**'Brown', huh?**

JOE
*Legging it around second—*

PAUL *(off)*
*Who's Joe Jackson?*

RED *(off)*

**He was one of the guys that threw the Series back in '19.**

CLOSE UP ON BUCK

*Watching, listening, as we slowly ZOOM IN on his face.*

BUD

**Guy like Jackson, he's not gonna come all the way up here just to play *baseball*.**

RED

**He was one of the Black Sox, kid.**

JOE

*Pulling into third base. He tips his hat and smiles shyly as the spectators APPLAUD. We SLOW ZOOM IN on him, then slowly FADE TO BLACK. A slow version of "After You've Gone" comes on the TRACK as the CREDITS ROLL on black next to insert shots of each of the banned players in better days, moving in slow-motion, smiling—playing ball.*

[1988]

# THE CELEBRATED JUMPING FROG OF CALAVERAS COUNTY

## Mark Twain

THERE WAS A FELLER HERE ONCE BY THE NAME OF JIM SMILEY, in the winter of '49—or maybe it was the spring of '50—I don't recollect exactly, somehow, though what makes me think it was one or the other is because I remember the big flume wasn't finished when he first came to the camp; but anyway, he was the curiousest man about always betting on anything that turned up you ever see, if he could get anybody to bet on the other side; and if he couldn't, he'd change sides. Any way that suited the other man would suit him—any way just so's he got a bet, *he* was satisfied. But still he was lucky, uncommon lucky; he most always come out winner. He was always ready and laying for a chance; there couldn't be no solit'ry thing mentioned but that feller'd offer to bet on it, and take any side you please, as I was just telling you. If there was a horse race, you'd find him flush, or you'd find him busted at the end of it; if there was a dogfight, he'd bet on it; if there was a cat-fight, he'd bet on it; if there was a chicken-fight, he'd bet on it; why, if there was two birds setting on a fence, he would bet you which one would fly first; or if there was a camp meeting, he would be there reg'lar, to bet on Parson Walker, which he judged to be the best exhorter about here, and so he was, too, and a good man. If he even seen a straddlebug start to go anywheres, he would bet you how long it would take him to get wherever he was going to, and if you took him up, he would foller that straddlebug to Mexico but what he would find out where he was bound for and how long he was on the road. Lots of the boys here has seen that Smiley, and can tell you about him. Why, it never made no difference to *him*—he would bet on *any*thing—the dangdest feller. Parson Walker's wife laid very sick once, for a good while, and it seemed as if they warn't going to save her; but one morning he come in, and Smiley asked how she was, and he said she was considerable better—thank the Lord for his inf'nit mercy—and coming on so smart that, with the blessing of Prov'dence, she'd get well yet; and Smiley, before he thought, says, "Well, I'll risk two-and-a-half that she don't, anyway."

Thish-yer Smiley had a mare—the boys called her the fifteen-minute nag, but that was only in fun, you know, because, of course, she was faster than that—and he used to win money on that horse, for all she was so slow and always had the asthma, or the distemper, or the consumption, or something of that kind. They used to give her two or three hundred yards start, and then pass her under way; but always at the fag end of the race she'd get excited and desperate-like, and come cavorting and straddling up, and scattering her legs around limber, sometimes in the air, and sometimes out to one side amongst the fences, and kicking up m-o-r-e dust, and raising m-o-r-e racket with her coughing and sneezing and blowing her nose—and always fetch up at the stand just about a neck ahead, as near as you could cipher it down.

And he had a little small bull pup, that to look at him you'd think he wan't worth a cent, but to set around and look ornery, and lay for a chance to steal something. But as soon as money was up on him, he was a different dog; his underjaw'd begin to stick out like the fo'castle of a steamboat, and his teeth would uncover, and shine savage like the furnaces. And a dog might tackle him, and bully-rag him, and bite him, and throw him over his shoulder two or three times, and Andrew Jackson—which was the name of the pup—Andrew Jackson would never let on but what *he* was satisfied, and hadn't expected nothing else—and the bets being doubled and doubled on the other side all the time, till the money was all up;

and then all of a sudden he would grab that other dog jest by the j'int of his hind leg and freeze to it—not chaw, you understand, but only jest grip and hang on till they throwed up the sponge, if it was a year. Smiley always come out winner on that pup, till he harnessed a dog once that didn't have no hind legs, because they'd been sawed off by a circular saw, and when the thing had gone along far enough, and the money was all up, and he come to make a snatch for his pet holt, he saw in a minute how he'd been imposed on, and how the other dog had him in the door, so to speak, and he 'peared surprised, and then he looked sorter discouraged-like, and didn't try no more to win the fight, and so he got shucked out bad. He give Smiley a look, as much as to say his heart was broke, and it was *his* fault for putting up a dog that hadn't no hind legs for him to take holt of, which was his main dependence in a fight, and then he limped off a piece and laid down and died. It was a good pup, was that Andrew Jackson, and would have made a name for hisself if he'd lived, for the stuff was in him, and he had genius—I know it, because he hadn't had no opportunities to speak of, and it don't stand to reason that a dog could make such a fight as he could under them circumstances, if he hadn't no talent. It always makes me feel sorry when I think of that last fight of his'n, and the way it turned out.

Well, thish-yer Smiley had rat-tarriers, and chicken cocks, and tomcats, and all them kind of things, till you couldn't rest, and you couldn't fetch nothing for him to bet on but he'd match you. He ketched a frog one day, and took him home, and said he cal'klated to edercate him; and so he never done nothing for three months but set in his back yard and learn that frog to jump. And you bet you he *did* learn him, too. He'd give him a little punch behind, and the next minute you'd see that frog whirling in the air like a doughnut—see him turn one summerset, or may be a couple, if he got a good start, and come down flatfooted and all right, like a cat. He got up so in the matter of catching flies, and kept him in practice so constant, that he'd nail a fly every time as far as he could see him. Smiley said all a frog wanted was education, and he could do most anything—and I believe him. Why, I've seen him set Dan'l Webster down here on this floor—Dan'l Webster was the name of the frog—and sing out, "Flies, Dan'l, flies!" and quicker'n you could wink, he'd spring straight up, and snake a fly off'n the counter there, and flop down on the floor again as solid as a gob of mud, and fall to scratching the side of his head with his hind foot as indifferent as if he hadn't no idea he'd been doin' any more'n any frog might do. You never see a frog so modest and straightfor'ard as he was, for all he was so gifted. And when it come to fair and square jumping on a dead level, he could get over more ground at one straddle than any animal of his breed you ever see. Jumping on a dead level was his strong suit, you understand; and when it come to that, Smiley would ante up money on him as long as he had a red. Smiley was monstrous proud of his frog, and well he might be, for fellers that had traveled and been everywheres, all said he laid over any frog that ever *they* see.

Well, Smiley kept the beast in a little lattice box, and he used to fetch him downtown sometimes and lay for a bet. One day a feller—a stranger in the camp, he was—come across him with his box, and says:

"What might it be that you've got in the box?"

And Smiley says, sorter indifferent like, "It might be a parrot, or it might be a canary, maybe, but it an't—it's only just a frog."

And the feller took it, and looked at it careful, and turned it round this way and that, and says, "H'm—so 'tis. Well, what's *he* good for?"

"Well," Smiley says, easy and careless, "he's good enough for *one* thing, I should judge—he can outjump any frog in Calaveras county."

The feller took the box again, and took another long, particular look, and give it back to Smiley, and says, very deliberate, "Well, I don't see no p'ints about that frog that's any better'n any other frog."

"Maybe you don't," Smiley says. "Maybe you understand frogs, and maybe you don't understand 'em; maybe you've had experience, and maybe you an't only a amature, as it were. Anyways, I've got *my* opinion, and I'll risk forty dollars that he can outjump any frog in Calaveras county."

And the feller studied a minute, and then says, kinder sad like, "Well, I'm only a stranger here, and I an't got no frog; but if I had a frog, I'd bet you."

And then Smiley says, "That's all right—that's all right—if you'll hold my box a minute, I'll go and get you a frog." And so the feller took the box, and put up his forty dollars along with Smiley's, and set down to wait.

So he set there a good while thinking and thinking to hisself, and then he got the frog out and prized his mouth open and took a teaspoon and filled him full of quail shot—filled him pretty near up to his chin—and set him on the floor. Smiley he went to the swamp and slopped around in the mud for a long time, and finally he ketched a frog, and fetched him in, and give him to the feller, and says:

"Now, if you're ready, set him alongside of Dan'l, with his fore-paws just even with Dan'l, and I'll give the word." Then he says, "One—two—three—jump!" and him and the feller touched up the frogs from behind, and the new frog hopped off, but Dan'l give a heave, and hysted up his shoulders—so—like a Frenchman, but it wan't no use—he couldn't budge; he was planted as solid as an anvil, and he couldn't no more stir than if he was anchored out. Smiley was a good deal surprised, and he was disgusted too, but he didn't have no idea what the matter was, of course.

The feller took the money and started away; and when he was going out at the door, he sorter jerked his thumb over his shoulders—this way—at Dan'l, and says again, very deliberate, "Well, *I* don't see no p'ints about that frog that's any better'n any other frog."

Smiley he stood scratching his head and looking down at Dan'l a long time, and at last he says, "I do wonder what in the nation that frog throw'd off for—I wonder if there an't something the matter with him—he 'pears to look mighty baggy, somehow." And he ketched Dan'l by the nap of the neck, and lifted him up and says, "Why, blame my cats, if he don't weigh five pound!" and turned him upside down, and he belched out a double handful of shot. And then he sees how it was, and he was the maddest man—he set the frog down and took out after that feller, but he never ketched him.

[1867]

# HER LETTERS

## Kate Chopin

SHE HAD GIVEN ORDERS THAT SHE WISHED TO REMAIN UNDISturbed and moreover had locked the doors of her room.

The house was very still. The rain was falling steadily from a leaden sky in which there was no gleam, no rift, no promise. A generous wood fire had been lighted in the ample fireplace and it brightened and illumined the luxurious apartment to its furthermost corner.

From some remote nook of her writing desk the woman took a thick bundle of letters, bound tightly together with strong, coarse twine, and placed it upon the table in the centre of the room.

For weeks she had been schooling herself for what she was about to do. There was a strong deliberation in the lines of her long, thin, sensitive face; her hands, too, were long and delicate and blue-veined.

With a pair of scissors she snapped the cord binding the letters together. Thus released the ones which were top-most slid down to the table and she, with a quick movement thrust her fingers among them, scattering and turning them over till they quite covered the broad surface of the table.

Before her were envelopes of various sizes and shapes, all of them addressed in the handwriting of one man and one woman. He had sent her letters all back to her one day when, sick with dread of possibilities, she had asked to have them returned. She had meant, then, to destroy them all, his and her own. That was four years ago, and she had been feeding upon them ever since; they had sustained her, she believed, and kept her spirit from perishing utterly.

But now the days had come when the premonition of danger could no longer remain unheeded. She knew that before many months were past she would have to part from her treasure, leaving it unguarded. She shrank from inflicting the pain, the anguish which the discovery of those letters would bring to others; to one, above all, who was near to her, and whose tenderness and years of devotion had made him, in a manner, dear to her.

She calmly selected a letter at random from the pile and cast it into her roaring fire. A second one followed almost as calmly, with the third her hand began to tremble; when, in a sudden paroxysm she cast a fourth, a fifth, and a sixth into the flames in breathless succession.

Then she stopped and began to pant—for she was far from strong, and she stayed staring into the fire with pained and savage eyes. Oh, what had she done! What had she not done! With feverish apprehension she began to search among the letters before her. Which of them had she so ruthlessly, so cruelly put out of her existence? Heaven grant, not the first, that very first one, written before they had learned, or dared to say to each other 'I love you'. No, no; there it was, safe enough. She laughed with pleasure, and held it to her lips. But what if that other most precious and most imprudent one were missing! in which every word of untempered passion had long ago eaten its way into her brain; and which stirred her still to-day, as it had done a hundred times before when she thought of it. She crushed it between her palms when she found it. She kissed it again and again. With her sharp white teeth she tore the far corner from the letter, where the name was written; she bit the torn scrap and tasted it between her lips and upon her tongue like some god-given morsel.

What unbounded thankfulness she felt at not having destroyed them all! How desolate and empty would have been her remaining days without them; with only her thoughts, illusive thoughts that she could not hold in her hands and press, as she did these, to her cheeks and her heart.

This man had changed the water in her veins to wine, whose taste had brought delirium to both of them. It was all one and past now, save for these letters that she held encircled in her arms. She stayed breathing softly and contentedly, with the hectic cheek resting upon them.

She was thinking, thinking of a way to keep them without possible ultimate injury to that other one whom they would stab more cruelly than keen knife blades.

At last she found the way. It was a way that frightened and bewildered her to think of at first, but she had reached it by deduction too sure to admit of doubt. She meant, of course, to destroy them herself before the end came. But how does the end come and when? Who may tell? She would guard against the possibility of accident by leaving them in charge of the very one who, above all, should be spared a knowledge of their contents.

She roused herself from the stupor of thought and gathered the scattered letters once more together, binding them again with the rough twine. She wrapped the compact bundle in a thick sheet of white polished paper. Then she wrote in ink upon the back of it, in large, firm characters:

'I leave this package to the care of my husband. With perfect faith in his loyalty and his love, I ask him to destroy it unopened.'

It was not sealed; only a bit of string held the wrapper, which she could remove and replace at will whenever the humor came to her to pass an hour in some intoxicating dream of the days when she felt she had lived.

[1894]

# UNCLE HAROLD

## Russell Baker

UNCLE HAROLD WAS FAMOUS FOR LYING.

He had once been shot right between the eyes. He told me so himself. It was during World War I. An underaged boy, he had run away from home, enlisted in the Marine Corps, and been shipped to France, where one of the Kaiser's soldiers had shot him. Right between the eyes.

It was a miracle it hadn't killed him, and I said so the evening he told me about it. He explained that Marines were so tough they didn't need miracles. I was now approaching the age of skepticism, and though it was risky business challenging adults, I was tempted to say, "Swear on the Bible?" I did not dare go this far, but I did get a hint of doubt into my voice by repeating his words as a question.

"Right between the eyes?"

"Right between the eyes," he said. "See this scar?"

He placed a finger on his forehead just above the bridge of his nose. "That's all the mark it left," he said.

"I don't see any scar," I said.

"It's probably faded by now," he said. "It's been a long time ago."

I said it must have hurt a good bit.

"Hurt! You bet it hurt."

"What did you do?"

"It made me so mad I didn't do a thing but pull out my pistol and kill that German right there on the spot."

At this point Aunt Sister came in from the kitchen with cups of cocoa. "For God's sake, Harold," she said, "quit telling the boy those lies."

People were always telling Uncle Harold for God's sake quit telling those lies. His full name was Harold Sharp, and in the family, people said, "That Harold Sharp is the biggest liar God ever sent down the pike."

Aunt Sister, Ida Rebecca's only daughter, had married him shortly after my mother took Doris and me from Morrisonville. He'd spent sixteen years in the Marines by then, but at Aunt Sister's insistence he gave up the Marine Corps and the two of them moved to Baltimore. There they had a small apartment on Hollins Street overlooking Union Square. Our place was a second-floor apartment on West Lombard Street just across the square. It was easy for my mother to stroll over to Aunt Sister's with Doris and me to play Parcheesi or Caroms or Pick-Up-Sticks with the two of them, but the real pleasure of these visits for me came from listening to Uncle Harold.

It didn't matter that my mother called him "the biggest liar God ever sent down the pike." In spite of his reputation for varnishing a fact, or maybe because of the outrageousness with which he did the varnishing, I found him irresistible. It was his intuitive refusal to spoil a good story by slavish adherence to fact that enchanted me. Though poorly educated, Uncle Harold somehow knew that the possibility of creating art lies not in reporting but in fiction.

He worked at cutting grass and digging graves for a cemetery in West Baltimore. This increased the romantic aura through which I saw him, for I had become fascinated with the Gothic aspects of death since arriving in Baltimore. In Baltimore, disposing of the dead seemed to be a major cultural activity. There were three funeral parlors within a one-block radius of our house, and a steady stream of hearses purred through the neighborhood. I had two other distant relatives from Morrisonville who had migrated to Baltimore, and both of them were also working in cemeteries. In addition, there was a fairly steady flow of corpses through our house on Lombard Street.

Our landlord there, a genial Lithuanian tailor who occupied

the first floor, lent out his parlor to a young relative who was an undertaker and sometimes had an overflow at his own establishment. As a result there was often an embalmed body coffined lavishly in the first-floor parlor. Since our apartment could be reached only by passing the landlord's parlor, and since its double doors were always wide open, it seemed to me that instead of finding a home of our own, we had come to rest in a funeral home. Passing in and out of the house, I tried to avert my eyes from the garishly rouged bodies and hold my breath against inhaling the cloying odors of candle wax, tuberoses, and embalming fluid which suffused the hallway.

When Uncle Harold came over for an evening of card playing and found a corpse in the parlor, his imagination came alive. On one such evening I went down to let Aunt Sister and him in the front door. Noting the coffin in our landlord's parlor, Uncle Harold paused, strode into the room, nodded at the mourners, and examined the deceased stranger with professional scrutiny. Upstairs afterwards, playing cards at the dining-room table, Uncle Harold announced that the old gentleman in the coffin downstairs did not look dead to him.

"I could swear I saw one of his eyelids flicker," he said.

Nobody paid him any attention.

"You can't always be sure they're dead," he said.

Nobody was interested except me.

"A man I knew was almost buried alive once," he said.

"Are you going to play the jack or hold it all night?" my mother asked.

"It was during the war," Uncle Harold said. "In France. They were closing the coffin on him when I saw him blink one eye."

The cards passed silently and were shuffled.

"I came close to being buried alive myself one time," he said.

"For God's sake, Harold, quit telling those lies," Aunt Sister said.

"It's the truth, just as sure as I'm sitting here, so help me

God," said Uncle Harold. "It happens every day. We dig them up out at the cemetery—to do autopsies, you know—and you can see they fought like the devil to get out after the coffin was closed on them, but it's too late by that time."

Uncle Harold was not a tall man, but the Marines had taught him to carry himself with a swaggering erect indolence and to measure people with the grave, cool arrogance of authority. Though he now shoveled dirt for a living, he was always immaculately manicured by the time he sat down to supper. In this polished man of the world—suits pressed to razor sharpness, every hair in place, eyes of icy gray self-confidence—I began to detect a hidden boy, in spirit not too different from myself, though with a love for mischief which had been subdued in me by too much melancholy striving to satisfy my mother's notions of manhood.

Admiring him so extravagantly, I was disappointed to find that he detested my hero, Franklin Roosevelt. In Uncle Harold's view, Roosevelt was a deep-dyed villain of the vilest sort. He had data about Roosevelt's shenanigans which newspapers were afraid to publish and occasionally entertained with hair-raising accounts of Rooseveltian deeds that had disgraced the Presidency.

"You know, I suppose, that Roosevelt only took the job for the money," he told me one evening.

"Does it pay a lot?"

"Not all that much," he said, "but there are plenty of ways of getting rich once you get in the White House, and Roosevelt's using all of them."

"How?"

"He collects money from everybody who wants to get in to see him"

"People have to give him money before he'll talk to them?"

"They don't give him the money face to face. He's too smart for that," Uncle Harold said.

"Then how does he get it?"

"There's a coat rack right outside his door, and he keeps an overcoat hanging on that rack. Before anybody can get in to see him, they've got to put money in the overcoat pocket."

I was shocked, which pleased Uncle Harold. "That's the kind of President you've got," he said.

"Do you know that for sure?"

"Everybody knows it."

"How do *you* know it?"

"A fellow who works at the White House told me how it's done."

This was such powerful stuff that as soon as I got home I passed it on to my mother. "Who told you that stuff?" she asked.

"Uncle Harold."

She laughed at my gullibility. "Harold Sharp is the biggest liar God ever sent down the pike," she said. "He doesn't know any more about Roosevelt than a hog knows about holiday."

Through Uncle Harold I first heard of H. L. Mencken. Mencken's house lay just two doors from Uncle Harold's place on Hollins Street. Uncle Harold pointed it out to me one day when we were walking around to the Arundel Ice Cream store for a treat. "You know who lives in that house, don't you?"

Of course I didn't.

"H. L. Mencken."

Who's H. L. Mencken?

"You mean to tell me you never heard of H. L. Mencken? He writes those pieces in the newspaper that make everybody mad," Uncle Harold said.

I understood from Uncle Harold's respectful tone that Mencken must be a great man, though Mencken's house did not look like the house of a great man. It looked very much like every other house in Baltimore. Red brick, white marble steps. "I saw Mencken coming out of his house just the other day," Uncle Harold said.

It's doubtful Uncle Harold had ever read anything by Mencken. Uncle Harold's tastes ran to *Doc Savage* and *The Shadow*. Still, I could see he was proud of living so close to such a great man. It was a measure of how well he had done in life at a time when millions of other men had been broken by the Depression.

He had left home in 1917 for the Marines, an uneducated fifteen-year-old country boy from Taylorstown, a village not far from Morrisonville, just enough schooling to read and do arithmetic, not much to look forward to but a career of farm labor. Maybe in the Marines he even became a hero. He did fight in France and afterwards stayed on in the Marines, shipping around the Caribbean under General Smedley Butler to keep Central America subdued while Yankee corporations pumped out its wealth. For a man with negligible expectations, he had not done badly by 1937 standards. Full-time cemetery labor; a one-bedroom apartment so close to a famous writer.

My first awe of him had softened as I gradually realized his information was not really intended to be information. Gradually I came to see that Uncle Harold was not a liar but a teller of stories and a romantic, and it was Uncle Harold the teller of tales who fascinated me. Though he remained a stern figure, and I never considered sassing him, I saw now that he knew I no longer received his stories with total credulity, but that I was now listening for the pleasure of watching his imagination at play. This change in our relationship seemed to please him.

Over the Parcheesi board one evening he told a story about watching the dead in Haiti get up out of their shrouds and dance the Charleston. Aunt Sister and my mother had the usual response: "For God's sake, Harold, quit telling those lies."

His face was impassive as always when he issued the usual

protest—"It's the truth, so help me God"—but I could see with absolute clarity that underneath the impassive mask he was smiling. He saw me studying him, scowled forbiddingly at me for one moment, then winked. That night we came to a silent understanding: We were two romancers whose desire for something more fanciful than the humdrum of southwest Baltimore was beyond the grasp of unimaginative people like Aunt Sister and my mother.

Still, it took me a while to understand what he was up to. He wanted life to be more interesting than it was, but his only gift for making it so lay in a small talent for homespun fictions, and he could not resist trying to make the most of it. Well, there was nothing tragic about his case. Our world in Baltimore hadn't much respect for the poetic impulse. In our world a man spinning a romance was doomed to be dismissed as nothing more than a prodigious liar.

It was common for the poorest household to contain a large dictionary, for conversation was a popular Depression pastime and Americans were passionately interested in words. Uncle Harold consulted his dictionary regularly looking for jaw-breaker vocabulary to give his tales more weight. One evening when my mother was there he made the mistake, when she spilled her cocoa, of saying that the spilled cocoa was "super-flu-us." Always the schoolmarm when it came to words, my mother chided him for ignorance. The word "superfluous," she pointed out, was ridiculously misused when talking about fluid on the tablecloth and, in any case, was not pronounced "super-flu-us."

Uncle Harold was often subjected to these small humiliations and accepted them without anger or sulkiness, at least when they came from women. Ungallant behavior toward a woman was not in his nature. This probably accounted for the happiness of his marriage, because Aunt Sister had inherited her mother's disposition to be a commander of men. Like her mother, Aunt Sister was tall, angular, tart, and forceful. Uncle Harold may have been the Marine by profession, but Aunt Sister was born and bred to be commandant of the household corps.

She had no patience for what she called Uncle Harold's "foolishness": his love of fiction, his habit of giving her romantic presents like filmy nightgowns and Evening in Paris perfume. She stored the cosmetics in a closet for use on special occasions which never arose and folded the lingerie away in chests where it lay forgotten. "Aunt Sister is too practical sometimes," said my mother, who thought Uncle Harold "a good man" despite his frailties, and therefore a man who deserved more indulgence than Aunt Sister granted him.

Without children of their own, Aunt Sister and Uncle Harold had chosen my sister, Doris, to love as dearly as the child they would never have. During our New Jersey years they had twice kept Doris with them in Baltimore during her summer vacations. These summers Uncle Harold stuffed Doris with ice cream and watermelon, rode the Ferris wheel with her at street carnivals, and entertained her with stories of gigantic serpents he'd fought in tropical jungles and cars he'd rolled over at a hundred miles an hour on the highway without denting a fender or ruffling a hair on his head.

Doris's heart belonged to Uncle Harold ever afterwards. Long after this time when he was young and she was a child, she was to discover that the ability of the true liar, which is the ability to lie to yourself, was not in him. He was to suffer a series of heart attacks so severe that only Aunt Sister and Doris were allowed at his hospital bedside. One night, trying to cheer him, Doris said, "The doctors say you're doing wonderfully. You'll be out of here and up and around in a couple of weeks now."

The true ability to lie was not in him. "You know it's no use," he said, which was the truth. He died two days later.

But that was in a time far beyond those years when he was showing me the pleasures to be had from setting imagination—even a limited imagination—free to play. To me he was the man playing Parcheesi and drinking cocoa in a two-room flat so close to H. L. Mencken, the man who infected me with the notion that there might be worse things to do with life than spend it in telling tales.

To me he was the man who could remember being born. He told me about it one night while Aunt Sister was out in the kitchen making cocoa. He could remember the very instant of birth. His mother was pleased, and the doctor who delivered him—Uncle Harold could remember this distinctly—said "It's a boy." There were several people in the room, and they all smiled at him. He could remember their faces vividly. And he smiled back.

[1993]

# CONFESSIONS OF
# A TAX CHEAT

## Jon Carroll

THANK HEAVENS THE IRS IS FINALLY CRACKING DOWN ON free-lance writers. For too long have these parasites been allowed to live high on the hog (or at least halfway up the hog) at the expense of honest wage earners.

Free-lance writers get to spend entire days in their bathrobes while others are dressing for success. They get to stay home while less fortunate citizens must brave the daily commute.

If you've ever seen a free-lance writer at work, you already know that most of his or her time is spent staring at cracks in the ceiling and trying to form animal faces out of them.

"If you squint, you can see a bear," a free-lance writer will tell the first person who comes along. This is a day's work for a free-lance writer.

And free-lance writers get to work for some of the noblest people in this nation: magazine editors. In 1935, a feature article in a national magazine would be worth (to the writer of said article) about $5000.

Today, 52 years later, a feature article in a national magazine is still worth about $5000.

Magazine editors have controlled the inflationary spiral. Politicians in Washington may spend money like water, but not magazine editors. They've been willing to make the hard choices.

Not that the free-lance writers were any help. All they did was whine.

Justice, however, has finally prevailed. The new tax code specifically and harshly limits the amount of deductions free-lance writers can take. It says, in essence, that a project must make money before deductions can be taken for expenses.

That right there eliminates 98 percent of the free-lance writers in this country. The point of free-lance writing is not to make money. The point of free-lance writing is to wear a bathrobe in the afternoon.

I have myself been a free-lance writer, and I know the kind of blatant cheating that goes on. I shudder to confess that I have done it myself.

For instance, stamps. I deducted the cost of stamps, because I had to mail my query letters and manuscripts and revisions and second revisions and letters inquiring about payment and further letters inquiring about payment and angry letters demanding payment; all the cost of doing business.

But some of the stamps I used for personal correspondence or bills or sweepstakes entries. Some of the stamps I just plain lost. And yet I deducted them.

Of course, since I only made $11,000 that year, the loss to the taxpayers was not significant. But it's the principle of the thing. And the interest, of course, except we're way beyond the statute of limitations.

And typing paper. I used some of that typing paper to mop up spilled glasses of pear nectar. Pear nectar takes a lot of paper, every single sheet fully deducted.

Multiply my bogus deductions by the number of free-lance writers in the nation (seems like about 100 million), and the cost to the American treasury is incalculable, at least by a free-lance writer.

Now that the IRS has finally nailed free-lance writers, I hope it will turn its attention to the really big fish in the tax-avoidance pond: the conceptual artists. You know, the my-life-is-my-art crowd. Forget Ivan Boesky; go after the folks who charge $5 to watch them kiss Chevrolets.

[1993]

# TAKING THE LIE DETECTOR

## John Dean

I TOOK CHARLIE STEP BY STEP THROUGH MY DEALINGS WITH the President on the cover-up, from the first meeting, on September 15, 1972, through the last. Charlie's cigar went out somewhere along the line, but he didn't notice.

"What do you think?" I asked finally.

Charlie stood up and walked across the room. He stopped and turned. His head was shaking and his lips were tight, as if they were fighting to hold back the words: "The President is a goddam criminal, that's what I think."

I nodded.

Charlie began pacing. "Now, listen, I want to go back over a couple of points. I want you to tell me again what he said about it being no problem to get a million bucks, and what you told him about laundering money. That's the damndest conversation I ever heard. The P sounds like the Godfather, for Christ's sake."

He sat back down in the easy chair beside our fireplace and listened as I repeated the conversation.

"Now tell me about the clemency offers again," he said.

I repeated it.

"The P's in trouble. Big trouble," he concluded and was off pacing again. Then, as he lit his cigar, "The P needs a lawyer and he better get himself a good one."

"Well, now you can understand why I suggested that Silbert and Glanzer get that tape of my meeting with Nixon on April fifteenth," I said.

"Yeah, I see." Charlie sat down again with a sigh. He was quiet for a long time. When he finally spoke, his mood had

changed. "I don't think I ever told you this, but I voted for
Nixon the last time. Everybody, I guess, figures that an old
Kennedy Democrat like me would love to nail Nixon, but I'd
figured the bastard would make a better President than
McGovern. You know," he continued as he watched the
smoke from his cigar swirl up toward the lamp beside him,
"it's damn depressing, what you just told me." He was silent
again.

"Would you like a drink?" Mo asked Charlie as she came
down the stairs to check on us.

"I'll have a little brandy if you've got some, thanks."
Charlie waited until she was out of the room and then spoke
to me softly. "I don't think you ought to tell McCandless
about the P. I don't think this stuff should be leaked to the
press. He'll learn about it in due time, but not now. Okay?"

"I agree."

Charlie sighed again. "You against the President. Shit, I
can't believe it. I knew you were carrying a load around in
your head, but I didn't realize it was a goddam atom bomb. I
want to think about this for a while. We're going to take this
one step at a time. It may be your word against Nixon's and
the rest of 'em, and that doesn't make me very comfortable."

"It doesn't make me very comfortable, either."

"Not that I don't believe you," Charlie reassured me, and I
knew he meant it.

He had said the same thing to me a few weeks earlier, at a
time when he had had doubts. It had been an awkward situation for him and most uncomfortable for me. I had gone to
his office to meet with him and had found that something was
bothering him. "I had a talk today with Silbert and Glanzer,"
he had said. "John, they don't believe your story about Gray
destroying documents, which makes them very leery of what
else you told them." Charlie's worried tone upset me. He
always sounded confident about everything. "They say
Petersen talked to Gray, and Gray has denied ever receiving

LYING, CHEATING & STEALING

any documents from you or Ehrlichman, let alone destroying them." Charlie shifted in his chair. "Now, I believe you," he added hastily, "but . . ." He was struggling for the right words. I knew my face must be registering my concern, and Charlie was trying to comfort me, but his words didn't offer solace. ". . . but I'm not the prosecutor in this case."

"Charlie, I'm telling you the truth. Gray told me he'd destroyed those documents. I'd swear to it under oath," I pleaded, looking for stronger assurance than the mere fact that my own lawyer believed me.

"Here's the problem. They say, 'Why should we believe Dean?' You see, it's your word against his, and just because I tell them Gray's a damn liar doesn't help us a bit. We've got to convince them, and I've got an idea I'd like to run by you." Charlie was more fidgety than I'd ever seen him. He spun a pencil with his hand as he spoke.

"Sure," I said, but I felt desperate. I'd been trying to convince myself that if I said what had happened I'd be believed. Now even Charlie wants more, I thought.

"Here's what I'm thinking. You don't have to do this if you don't want to, but it might be a good idea if you took a lie-detector test. If the results don't come out right, we'll put the goddam report in the bottom drawer and bury it." Charlie was testing me.

"Hell, Charlie, I'm ready. Gray's lying, and if that's what I've got to do to prove it, fine."

"Terrific. That's terrific. I'll set it up for you as soon as we can do it. I've got the man." He was smiling for the first time since I had arrived, which made me feel better.

Charlie called a private investigator and made the arrangements. The next day I would "get on the box," as he called it.

Charlie's investigator friend and the lie-detector expert were waiting for me in the uninviting back room of a sterile prefabricated office building in suburban Maryland. What if

I fail, I kept thinking; then I'm going to be in really big trouble. I had nearly convinced myself that no machine could register anything about me because my central nervous system was carrying more voltage than it was built to handle. The tester tried to put me at ease. The purpose, he explained, was not to trick or surprise me. We reviewed the questions carefully.

There was no way to get comfortable in the hardwood chair, with terminals attached to my fingers, a blood-pressure tourniquet around one of my arms, and a rubber belt around my chest. Wires ran behind me to "the box." The tourniquet cut off the circulation in my arm. I felt a tingling feeling as my fingers fell asleep, then pain. This was normal, the tester said when I complained. He kept asking questions: "Did you turn documents from Hunt's safe over to Pat Gray? . . . Did Mr. Gray tell you he had destroyed the documents from Hunt's safe you had given him?"

"We're almost finished," he said. "But I want to do one more test. Please select a card." He held out a fan of half a dozen playing cards. "Now, remember the card you selected. I'm going to call off all the cards, and I want you to lie to me about which card you selected." He read off the cards and I picked the wrong one. He peered at his instruments, laughing. "That's a good sign. You damn near broke my machine when you lied." I felt better as he unhooked me from the straps and wires.

Charlie called when he received the report the next day. He was riding high again. "Son, from now on whenever there's any doubt about who's telling the truth, you're going to get on the box. I already called Silbert and told him to get Gray on the box, because my man passed with flying colors." Gray, of course, never took a lie-detector test; he finally confessed that he had destroyed the documents.

The polygraph test was not wasted. It led us to an important decision: I would testify only to facts on which I was prepared to take a lie-detector test. Often when we were preparing testimony in sensitive areas, Charlie would lean over, smiling, and ask whether I was ready to go on the box about it. It would give us a boost as we squared off against the President.

[1977]

# I'LL ALWAYS HAVE PARIS

## Art Buchwald

IT WAS IN ENGLAND THAT I GOT MY BEST SCAM STORY. IT took place at Cartier's on Bond Street in London. A well-dressed man came in and admired a necklace in the window that was priced at £150,000. He came in every day to look at it. As the weeks went by, the salespeople became used to his daily visits. Finally, on a Saturday morning, he said he'd take it. Would they accept a check? The salesperson nervously called his superior at home and asked for instructions. The superior told him to check with Claridge's Hotel, where the client was staying. Claridge's reported that the man had a large suite and seemed to be well off. So the decision was made to sell him the necklace.

An hour later, a man saying he was a pawnbroker called, and said that a well-dressed man had come in and offered to sell him a new Cartier's necklace for £20,000. The pawnbroker knew the piece was worth a lot more than that, and thought Cartier's should be alerted. All the alarm bells in Cartier's went off.

"Did he say where he was going?"

"He mentioned taking the ferry at Dover."

Cartier's called the police and asked them to pick up their customer, which they did. They found the necklace on him and he was thrown in jail for the weekend.

Now this is the part of the story I like the best. On Monday morning, the man's check proved to be good and cleared his bank. He sued for false arrest, and Cartier's had to settle for *twice* what the necklace was worth.

It was an inspired tale, and if anyone tries to steal the idea for a movie, I will sue him.

[1997]

# A RETRIEVED REFORMATION

## O. Henry

A GUARD CAME TO THE PRISON SHOE-SHOP, WHERE JIMMY Valentine was assiduously stitching uppers, and escorted him to the front office. There the warden handed Jimmy his pardon, which had been signed that morning by the governor. Jimmy took it in a tired kind of way. He had served nearly ten months of a four-year sentence. He had expected to stay only about three months, at the longest. When a man with as many friends on the outside as Jimmy Valentine had is received in the "stir" it is hardly worth while to cut his hair.

"Now, Valentine," said the warden, "you'll go out in the morning. Brace up, and make a man of yourself. You're not a bad fellow at heart. Stop cracking safes, and live straight."

"Me?" said Jimmy, in surprise. "Why, I never cracked a safe in my life."

"Oh, no," laughed the warden. "Of course not. Let's see, now. How was it you happened to get sent up on that Springfield job? Was it because you wouldn't prove an alibi for fear of compromising somebody in extremely high-toned society? Or was it simply a case of a mean old jury that had it in for you? It's always one or the other with you innocent victims."

"Me?" said Jimmy, still blankly virtuous. "Why, warden, I never was in Springfield in my life!"

"Take him back, Cronin," smiled the warden, "and fix him up with outgoing clothes. Unlock him at seven in the morning, and let him come to the bull-pen. Better think over my advice, Valentine."

At a quarter past seven on the next morning Jimmy stood in the warden's outer office. He had on a suit of the villainously fitting, ready-made clothes and a pair of the stiff, squeaky shoes that the state furnishes to its discharged compulsory guests.

The clerk handed him a railroad ticket and the five-dollar bill with which the law expected him to rehabilitate himself into good citizenship and prosperity. The warden gave him a cigar, and shook hands. Valentine, 9762, was chronicled on the books "Pardoned by Governor," and Mr. James Valentine walked out into the sunshine.

Disregarding the song of the birds, the waving green trees, and the smell of the flowers, Jimmy headed straight for a restaurant. There he tasted the first sweet joys of liberty in the shape of a broiled chicken and a bottle of white wine—followed by a cigar a grade better than the one the warden had given him. From there he proceeded leisurely to the depot. He tossed a quarter into the hat of a blind man sitting by the door, and boarded his train. Three hours set him down in a little town near the state line. He went to the café of one Mike Dolan and shook hands with Mike, who was alone behind the bar.

"Sorry we couldn't make it sooner, Jimmy, me boy," said Mike. "But we had that protest from Springfield to buck against, and the governor nearly balked. Feeling all right?"

"Fine," said Jimmy. "Got my key?"

He got his key and went upstairs, unlocking the door of a room at the rear. Everything was just as he had left it. There on the floor was still Ben Price's collar-button that had been torn from that eminent detective's shirt-band when they had overpowered Jimmy to arrest him.

Pulling out from the wall a folding-bed, Jimmy slid back a panel in the wall and dragged out a dust-covered suitcase. He opened this and gazed fondly at the finest set of burglar's tools in the East. It was a complete set, made of specially tempered steel, the latest designs in drills, punches, braces and bits, jimmies, clamps, and augers, with two or three novelties invented by Jimmy himself, in which he took pride. Over nine hundred dollars they had cost him to have made at ———, a place where they make such things for the profession.

In half an hour Jimmy went downstairs and through the café. He was now dressed in tasteful and well-fitting clothes, and carried his dusted and cleaned suitcase in his hand.

"Got anything on?" asked Mike Dolan, genially.

"Me?" said Jimmy, in a puzzled tone. "I don't understand. I'm representing the New York Amalgamated Short Snap Biscuit Cracker and Frazzled Wheat Company."

This statement delighted Mike to such an extent that Jimmy had to take a seltzer-and-milk on the spot. He never touched "hard" drinks.

A week after the release of Valentine, 9762, there was a neat job of safe-burglary done in Richmond, Indiana, with no clue to the author. A scant eight hundred dollars was all that was secured. Two weeks after that a patented, improved burglar-proof safe in Logansport was opened like a cheese to the tune of fifteen hundred dollars, currency; securities and silver untouched. That began to interest the rogue-catchers. Then an old-fashioned bank-safe in Jefferson City became active and threw out of its crater an eruption of bank-notes amounting to five thousand dollars. The losses were now high enough to bring the matter up into Ben Price's class of work. By comparing notes, a remarkable similarity in the methods of the burglaries was noticed. Ben Price investigated the scenes of the robberies, and was heard to remark:

"That's Dandy Jim Valentine's autograph. He's resumed business. Look at that combination knob—jerked out as easy as pulling up a radish in wet weather. He's got the only clamps that can do it. And look how clean those tumblers were punched out! Jimmy never has to drill but one hole. Yes, I guess I want Mr. Valentine. He'll do his bit next time without any short-time or clemency foolishness."

Ben Price knew Jimmy's habits. He had learned them while working up the Springfield case. Long jumps, quick

get-aways, no confederates, and a taste for good society—
these ways had helped Mr. Valentine to become noted as a
successful dodger of retribution. It was given out that Ben
Price had taken up the trail of the elusive cracksman, and
other people with burglar-proof safes felt more at ease.

One afternoon Jimmy Valentine and his suitcase climbed
out of the mail-hack in Elmore, a little town five miles off the
railroad down in the black-jack country of Arkansas. Jimmy,
looking like an athletic young senior just home from college,
went down the board sidewalk toward the hotel.

A young lady crossed the street, passed him at the corner
and entered a door over which was the sign "The Elmore
Bank." Jimmy Valentine looked into her eyes, forgot what he
was, and became another man. She lowered her eyes and colored slightly. Young men of Jimmy's style and looks were
scarce in Elmore.

Jimmy collared a boy that was loafing on the steps of the
bank as if he were one of the stock-holders, and began to ask
him questions about the town, feeding him dimes at intervals.
By and by the young lady came out, looking royally unconscious of the young man with the suitcase, and went her way.

"Isn't that young lady Miss Polly Simpson?" asked Jimmy,
with specious guile.

"Naw," said the boy. "She's Annabel Adams. Her pa owns
this bank. What'd you come to Elmore for? Is that a gold
watch-chain? I'm going to get a bulldog. Got any more
dimes?"

Jimmy went to the Planters' Hotel, registered as Ralph D.
Spencer, and engaged a room. He leaned on the desk and
declared his platform to the clerk. He said he had come to
Elmore to look for a location to go into business. How was
the shoe business, now, in the town? He had thought of the
shoe business. Was there an opening?

The clerk was impressed by the clothes and manner of
Jimmy. He, himself, was something of a pattern of fashion to

the thinly gilded youth of Elmore, but he now perceived his shortcomings. While trying to figure out Jimmy's manner of tying his four-in-hand, he cordially gave the information.

Yes, there ought to be a good opening in the shoe line. There wasn't an exclusive shoe-store in the place. The dry-goods and general stores handled them. Business in all lines was fairly good. Hoped Mr. Spencer would decide to locate in Elmore. He would find it a pleasant town to live in, and the people very sociable.

Mr. Spencer thought he would stop over in the town a few days and look over the situation. No, the clerk needn't call the boy. He would carry up his suitcase, himself; it was rather heavy.

Mr. Ralph Spencer, the phoenix that arose from Jimmy Valentine's ashes—ashes left by the flame of a sudden and alternative attack of love—remained in Elmore, and prospered. He opened a shoe-store and secured a good run of trade.

Socially he was also a success, and made many friends. And he accomplished the wish of his heart. He met Miss Annabel Adams, and became more and more captivated by her charms.

At the end of a year the situation of Mr. Ralph Spencer was this: he had won the respect of the community, his shoe-store was flourishing, and he and Annabel were engaged to be married in two weeks. Mr. Adams, the typical, plodding, country banker, approved of Spencer. Annabel's pride in him almost equalled her affection. He was as much at home in the family of Mr. Adams and that of Annabel's married sister as if he were already a member.

One day Jimmy sat down in his room and wrote this letter, which he mailed to the safe address of one of his old friends in St. Louis:

*Dear Old Pal:*

*I want you to be at Sullivan's place, in Little Rock, next Wednesday night at nine o'clock. I want you to wind up some little matters for me. And, also, I want to make you a present of my kit of tools. I know you'll be glad to get them—you couldn't duplicate the lot for a thousand dollars. Say, Billy, I've quit the old business—a year ago. I've got a nice store. I'm making an honest living, and I'm going to marry the finest girl on earth two weeks from now. It's the only life, Billy—the straight one. I wouldn't touch a dollar of another man's money now for a million. After I get married I'm going to sell out and go West, where there won't be so much danger of having old scores brought up against me. I tell you, Billy, she's an angel. She believes in me; and I wouldn't do another crooked thing for the whole world. Be sure to be at Sully's, for I must see you. I'll bring along the tools with me.*

*Your old friend,*
*Jimmy.*

On the Monday night after Jimmy wrote this letter, Ben Price jogged unobtrusively into Elmore in a livery buggy. He lounged about town in his quiet way until he found out what he wanted to know. From the drug-store across the street from Spencer's shoe-store he got a good look at Ralph D. Spencer.

"Going to marry the banker's daughter, are you, Jimmy?" said Ben to himself, softly. "Well, I don't know!"

The next morning Jimmy took his breakfast at the Adamses. He was going to Little Rock that day to order his wedding-suit and buy something nice for Annabel. That would be the first time he had left town since he came to Elmore. It had been more than a year now since those last professional "jobs," and he thought he could safely venture out.

After breakfast quite a family party went down town together—Mr. Adams, Annabel, Jimmy, and Annabel's married sister with her two little girls, aged five and nine. They came by the hotel where Jimmy still boarded, and he ran up to his room and brought along his suitcase. Then they went on to the bank. There stood Jimmy's horse and buggy and Dolph Gibson, who was going to drive him over to the railroad station.

All went inside the high, carved oak railings into the

banking-room—Jimmy included, for Mr. Adams's future son-in-law was welcome anywhere. The clerks were pleased to be greeted by the good-looking, agreeable young man who was going to marry Miss Annabel. Jimmy set his suitcase down. Annabel, whose heart was bubbling with happiness and lively youth, put on Jimmy's hat and picked up the suitcase. "Wouldn't I make a nice drummer?" said Annabel. "My! Ralph, how heavy it is. Feels like it was full of gold bricks."

"Lot of nickel-plated shoe-horns in there," said Jimmy, coolly, "that I'm going to return. Thought I'd save express charges by taking them up. I'm getting awfully economical."

The Elmore Bank had just put in a new safe and vault. Mr. Adams was very proud of it, and insisted on an inspection by every one. The vault was a small one, but it had a new patented door. It fastened with three solid steel bolts thrown simultaneously with a single handle, and had a time-lock. Mr. Adams beamingly explained its workings to Mr. Spencer, who showed a courteous but not too intelligent interest. The two children, May and Agatha, were delighted by the shining metal and funny clock and knobs.

While they were thus engaged Ben Price sauntered in and leaned on his elbow, looking casually inside between the railings. He told the teller that he didn't want anything; he was just waiting for a man he knew.

Suddenly there was a scream or two from the women, and a commotion. Unperceived by the elders, May, the nine-year-old girl, in a spirit of play, had shut Agatha in the vault. She had then shot the bolts and turned the knob of the combination as she had seen Mr. Adams do.

The old banker sprang to the handle and tugged at it for a moment. "The door can't be opened," he groaned. "The clock hasn't been wound nor the combination set."

Agatha's mother screamed again, hysterically.

"Hush!" said Mr. Adams, raising his trembling hand. "All be quiet for a moment. Agatha!" he called as loudly as he could. "Listen to me." During the following silence they could just hear the faint sound of the child wildly shrieking in the dark vault in a panic of terror.

"My precious darling!" wailed the mother. "She will die of fright! Open the door! Oh, break it open! Can't you men do something?"

"There isn't a man nearer than Little Rock who can open that door," said Mr. Adams, in a shaky voice. "My God! Spencer, what shall we do? That child—she can't stand it long in there. There isn't enough air, and, besides, she'll go into convulsions from fright."

Agatha's mother, frantic now, beat the door of the vault with her hands. Somebody wildly suggested dynamite. Annabel turned to Jimmy, her large eyes full of anguish, but not yet despairing. To a woman nothing seems quite impossible to the powers of the man she worships.

"Can't you do something, Ralph—*try*, won't you?"

He looked at her with a queer, soft smile on his lips and in his keen eyes.

"Annabel," he said, "give me that rose you are wearing, will you?"

Hardly believing that she heard him aright, she unpinned the bud from the bosom of her dress, and placed it in his hand. Jimmy stuffed it into his vest-pocket, threw off his coat and pulled up his shirt-sleeves. With that act Ralph D. Spencer passed away and Jimmy Valentine took his place.

"Get away from the door, all of you," he commanded, shortly.

He set his suitcase on the table, and opened it out flat. From that time on he seemed to be unconscious of the presence of any one else. He laid out the shining, queer implements swiftly and orderly, whistling softly to himself as he always did when at work. In a deep silence and immovable, the others watched him as if under a spell.

In a minute Jimmy's pet drill was biting smoothly into the

steel door. In ten minutes—breaking his own burglarious record—he threw back the bolts and opened the door.

Agatha, almost collapsed, but safe, was gathered into her mother's arms.

Jimmy Valentine put on his coat, and walked outside the railings toward the front door. As he went he thought he heard a far-away voice that he once knew call "Ralph!" But he never hesitated.

At the door a big man stood somewhat in his way.

"Hello, Ben!" said Jimmy, still with his strange smile. "Got around at last, have you? Well, let's go. I don't know that it makes much difference, now."

And then Ben Price acted rather strangely.

"Guess you're mistaken, Mr. Spencer," he said. "Don't believe I recognize you. Your buggy's waiting for you, ain't it?"

And Ben Price turned and strolled down the street.

[1909]

# THE WALTZ

## Dorothy Parker

*WHY, THANK YOU SO MUCH. I'D ADORE TO.*

I don't want to dance with him. I don't want to dance with anybody. And even if I did, it wouldn't be him. He'd be well down among the last ten. I've seen the way he dances; it looks like something you do on Saint Walpurgis Night. Just think, not a quarter of an hour ago, here I was sitting, feeling so sorry for the poor girl he was dancing with. And now *I'm* going to be the poor girl. Well, well. Isn't it a small world?

And a peach of a world, too. A true little corker. Its events are so fascinatingly unpredictable, are not they? Here I was, minding my own business, not doing a stitch of harm to any living soul. And then he comes into my life, all smiles and city manners, to sue me for the favor of one memorable mazurka. Why, he scarcely knows my name, let alone what it stands for. It stands for Despair, Bewilderment, Futility, Degradation, and Premeditated Murder, but little does he wot. I don't wot his name, either; I haven't any idea what it is. Jukes, would be my guess from the look in his eyes. How do you do, Mr. Jukes? And how is that dear little brother of yours, with the two heads?

Ah, now why did he have to come around me, with his low requests? Why can't he let me lead my own life? I ask so little—just to be left alone in my quiet corner of the table, to do my evening brooding over all my sorrows. And he must come, with his bows and his scrapes and his may-I-have-this-ones. And I had to go and tell him that I'd adore to dance with him. I cannot understand why I wasn't struck right down dead. Yes, and being struck dead would look like a day in the country, compared to struggling out a dance with this boy. But what could I do? Everyone else at the table had got up to dance, except him and me. There was I, trapped. Trapped like a trap in a trap.

What can you say, when a man asks you to dance with him? I most certainly will *not* dance with you, I'll see you in hell first. Why, thank you, I'd like to awfully, but I'm having labor pains. Oh, yes, *do* let's dance together—it's so nice to meet a man who isn't a scaredy-cat about catching my beri-beri. No. There was nothing for me to do, but say I'd adore to. Well, we might as well get it over with. All right, Cannonball, let's run out on the field. You won the toss; you can lead.

*Why, I think it's more of a waltz, really. Isn't it? We might just listen to the music a second. Shall we? Oh, yes, it's a waltz. Mind? Why, I'm simply thrilled. I'd love to waltz with you.*

I'd love to waltz with you. I'd love to waltz with you. I'd love to have my tonsils out, I'd love to be in a midnight fire at sea. Well, it's too late now. We're getting under way. *Oh.* Oh, dear. Oh, dear, dear, dear. Oh, this is even worse than I thought it would be. I suppose that's the one dependable law of life—everything is always worse than you thought it was going to be. Oh, if I had any real grasp of what this dance would be like, I'd have held out for sitting it out. Well, it will probably amount to the same thing in the end. We'll be sitting it out on the floor in a minute, if he keeps this up.

I'm so glad I brought it to his attention that this is a waltz they're playing. Heaven knows what might have happened, if he had thought it was something fast; we'd have blown the sides right out of the building. Why does he always want to be somewhere that he isn't? Why can't we stay in one place just long enough to get acclimated? It's this constant rush, rush, rush, that's the curse of American life. That's the reason that we're all of us so—*Ow!* For God's sake, don't *kick*, you idiot; this is only second down. Oh, my shin. My poor, poor shin, that I've had ever since I was a little girl!

*Oh, no, no, no. Goodness, no. It didn't hurt the least little bit.
And anyway it was my fault. Really it was. Truly. Well, you're just
being sweet, to say that. It really was all my fault.*

I wonder what I'd better do—kill him this instant, with my
naked hands, or wait and let him drop in his traces. Maybe it's
best not to make a scene. I guess I'll just lie low, and watch the
pace get him. He can't keep this up indefinitely—he's only
flesh and blood. Die he must, and die he shall, for what he did
to me. I don't want to be of the over-sensitive type, but you
can't tell me that kick was unpremeditated. Freud says there
are no accidents. I've led no cloistered life, I've known dancing partners who have spoiled my slippers and torn my dress;
but when it comes to kicking, I am Outraged Womanhood.
When you kick me in the shin, *smile.*

Maybe he didn't do it maliciously. Maybe it's just his way
of showing his high spirits. I suppose I ought to be glad that
one of us is having such a good time. I suppose I ought to
think myself lucky if he brings me back alive. Maybe it's cap-
tious to demand of a practically strange man that he leave your
shins as he found them. After all, the poor boy's doing the
best he can. Probably he grew up in the hill country, and
never had no larnin'. I bet they had to throw him on his back
to get shoes on him.

*Yes, it's lovely, isn't it? It's simply lovely. It's the loveliest waltz.
Isn't it? Oh, I think it's lovely, too.*

Why, I'm getting positively drawn to the Triple Threat
here. He's my hero. He has the heart of a lion, and the sinews
of a buffalo. Look at him—never a thought of the consequences, never afraid of his face, hurling himself into every
scrimmage, eyes shining, cheeks ablaze. And shall it be said that
I hung back? No, a thousand times no. What's it to me if I
have to spend the next couple of years in a plaster cast? Come
on, Butch, right through them! Who wants to live forever?

Oh, Oh, dear. Oh, he's all right, thank goodness. For a
while I thought they'd have to carry him off the field. Ah, I

couldn't bear to have anything happen to him. I love him. I love him better than anybody in the world. Look at the spirit he gets into a dreary, commonplace waltz; how effete the other dancers seem, beside him. He is youth and vigor and courage, he is strength and gaiety and—*Ow!* Get off my instep, you hulking peasant! What do you think I am, any-way—a gangplank? *Ow!*

*No, of course it didn't hurt. Why, it didn't a bit. Honestly. And it was all my fault. You see, that little step of yours—well, it's per-fectly lovely, but it's just a tiny bit tricky to follow at first. Oh, did you work it up yourself? You really did? Well, aren't you amazing! Oh, now I think I've got it. Oh, I think it's lovely. I was watching you do it when you were dancing before. It's awfully effective when you look at it.*

It's awfully effective when you look at it. I bet I'm awfully effective when you look at me. My hair is hanging along my cheeks, my skirt is swaddling about me, I can feel the cold damp of my brow. I must look like something out of "The Fall of the House of Usher." This sort of thing takes a fearful toll of a woman my age. And he worked up his little step himself, he with his degenerate cunning. And it was just a tiny bit tricky at first, but now I think I've got it. Two stum-bles, slip, and a twenty-yard dash; yes. I've got it. I've got several other things, too, including a split shin and a bitter heart. I hate this creature I'm chained to. I hated him the moment I saw his leering, bestial face. And here I've been locked in his noxious embrace for the thirty-five years this waltz has lasted. Is that orchestra never going to stop playing? Or must this obscene travesty of a dance go on until hell burns out?

*Oh, they're going to play another encore. Oh, goody. Oh, that's lovely. Tired? I should say I'm not tired. I'd like to go on like this forever.*

I should say I'm not tired. I'm dead, that's all I am. Dead, and in what a cause! And the music is never going to stop playing, and we're going on like this, Double-Time Charlie and I, throughout eternity. I suppose I won't care any more, after the first hundred thousand years. I suppose nothing will matter then, not heat nor pain nor broken heart nor cruel, aching weariness. Well. It can't come too soon for me.

I wonder why I didn't tell him I was tired. I wonder why I didn't suggest going back to the table. I could have said let's just listen to the music. Yes, and if he would, that would be the first bit of attention he has given it all evening. George Jean Nathan said that the lovely rhythms of the waltz should be listened to in stillness and not be accompanied by strange gyrations of the human body. I think that's what he said. I think it was George Jean Nathan. Anyhow, whatever he said and whoever he was and whatever he's doing now, he's better off than I am. That's safe. Anybody who isn't waltzing with this Mrs. O'Leary's cow I've got here is having a good time.

Still if we were back at the table, I'd probably have to talk to him. Look at him—what could you say to a thing like that! Did you go to the circus this year, what's your favorite kind of ice cream, how do you spell cat? I guess I'm as well off here. As well off as if I were in a cement mixer in full action.

I'm past all feeling now. The only way I can tell when he steps on me is that I can hear the splintering of bones. And all the events of my life are passing before my eyes. There was the time I was in a hurricane in the West Indies, there was the day I got my head cut open in the taxi smash, there was the night the drunken lady threw a bronze ash-tray at her own true love and got me instead, there was that summer that the sailboat kept capsizing. Ah, what an easy, peaceful time was mine, until I fell in with Swifty, here. I didn't know what trouble was, before I got drawn into this *danse macabre*. I think my mind is beginning to wander. It almost seems to me as if the orchestra were stopping. It couldn't be, of course; it could never, never be. And yet in my ears there is a silence like the sound of angel voices . . . .

*Oh, they've stopped, the mean things. They're not going to play any more. Oh, darn. Oh, do you think they would? Do you really think so, if you gave them twenty dollars? Oh, that would be lovely. And look, do tell them to play this same thing. I'd simply adore to go on waltzing.*

[1933]

# ACKNOWLEDGMENTS

# AUTHOR BIOGRAPHIES

**WOODY ALLEN** is best known for his film acting and directing, but he is also an accomplished playwright and author. His humor collections include *Getting Even, Without Feathers*, and *Side Effects*.

**RUSSELL BAKER** began his career as a police reporter for the *Baltimore Sun*. He has worked for the *New York Times* since 1954 and has won the Pulitzer prize twice.

**RUSSELL BANKS** is a poet, novelist, and short-story writer, and he teaches creative writing at Princeton University. His books include *Continental Drift, Success Stories, Family Life,* and *Rule of the Bone*.

**STANLEY BING** is a senior executive at a gigantic multinational corporation he refuses to name. He has been writing on corporate strategy since 1984, first in *Esquire* and more recently in *Fortune*.

**ART BUCHWALD** began writing his column for the *New York Herald Tribune* in 1949. He won the Pulitzer prize in 1982, and his column is syndicated internationally.

**JON CARROLL** began his career at the at the age of seventeen at the *San Francisco Chronicle*. Several decades later he continues to be a columnist for the *Chronicle*.

**KATE CHOPIN** began her writing career in 1884 after moving back to St. Louis with her six children following the death of her husband. Her novel *The Awakening* received a storm of negative criticism upon publication, but was rediscovered in the 1960s and is now her most popular work.

**e  e  cummings** was born in Cambridge, Massachusetts, and educated at Harvard University. He was an ambulance driver during World War I, then studied art in Paris after the war. An inventive and popular poet, he died in 1962.

**JOHN DEAN**, White House counsel during the Nixon administration, was at the center of the Watergate scandal that ended Nixon's presidency. He was dismissed as counsel in 1973 and years later consulted on Oliver Stone's controversial film *Nixon*.

**ERROL FLYNN** was born in 1909 in Tasmania, New Zealand. He was the swashbuckling star of 1930s' and 1940s' adventure films such as *Captain Blood* and *The Adventures of Robin Hood*. *My Wicked, Wicked Ways* was his only book.

**DASHIELL HAMMETT** was a detective for eight years after World War I, an experience that provided the inspiration for his many detective novels and his most legendary character, private eye Sam Spade.

**CYNTHIA HEIMEL** has written for *Playboy*, *Los Angeles Magazine,* and the *Village Voice*, and published several collections of essays, including *If You Leave, Can I Come Too?* and *When Your Phone Doesn't Ring, It Will Be Me.*

**O. HENRY** was convicted of embezzlement while working as a bank teller. After serving three years in a penitentiary, he settled in New York City and wrote short stories for popular magazines in the early 1900s.

**SHERE HITE** has produced three best-sellers about sex and love in the United States. Although her methodology and feminist approach have created controversy, *The Hite Report* has been compared with the groundbreaking research of Alfred Kinsey and Masters and Johnson.

**MARY KARR** is a prize-winning poet whose recent memoir, *The Liars' Club*, chronicles her childhood in an east Texas oil town.

**ANN LANDERS**, a pseudonym of Ester (Eppie) Pauline Friedman Lederer, has been writing her advice column since 1955. She is now syndicated in over 1,000 newspapers in America and abroad.

**MICHAEL LEWIS** grew up in New Orleans and holds degrees from Princeton and the London School of Economics. He has written for the *New Republic,* the *Economist,* and the *Wall Street Journal,* among other publications.

**GROUCHO MARX** was born Julius Marx in 1890, and, along with his three brothers, became a part of the well-known vaudeville and film act the Marx Brothers. He starred in the comedies *Animal Crackers, Duck Soup,* and *A Night at the Opera.*

**DOROTHY PARKER** wrote literary and dramatic criticism as well as short stories and verse. She is perhaps best remembered for her fabled wit at the Algonquin Round Table of the 1920s and 1930s.

**S. J. PERELMAN** was born in New York and attended Brown University. In addition to being a humorist, he also wrote screenplays and Broadway plays, including *One Touch of Venus* with Ogden Nash and Kurt Weill.

**KATHERINE ANNE PORTER** was born in Indian Creek, Texas, in 1890. She is considered one the masters of the short-story form, and she won a Pulitzer prize in 1966 for her *Collected Stories.* Her only novel, *Ship of Fools,* was made into a film in 1965.

**JOHN SAYLES** is perhaps best known for his film acting and directing in *Return of the Secaucus 7, Matewan,* and most recently, *Lone Star.* He has also won two O. Henry Awards for his short stories and published the novels *Pride of the Bimbos* and *Union Dues.*

**JAMES THURBER** was a member of the Algonquin Round Table and one of the mainstays of the *New Yorker,* where his short stories, essays, and cartoons were published for over thirty years.

**MARK TWAIN** was the pen name adopted by Samuel Clemens when he was a reporter for the Virginia City (Nevada) *Territorial Enterprise.* The celebrated author of *The Adventures of Huckleberry Finn, The Adventures of Tom Sawyer,* and other classics also displayed his stinging wit in his essays, letters, and speeches.

**GEOFFREY WOLFF** was born in Los Angeles in 1937 and educated at Princeton University. He has written several novels as well as the nonfiction *The Duke of Deception.* He currently teaches in the graduate fiction program at the University of California at Irvine.

**TOBIAS WOLFF** is a memoirist and fiction writer. His nonfiction work includes *This Boy's Life* and *In Pharaoh's Army: Memories of the Lost War.* "The Liar" originally appeared in the *Atlantic Monthly.*

**ALEXANDER WOOLLCOTT** was an author, critic, and actor known for his acerbic wit. In 1914 he started his journalism career as a cub reporter at the *New York Times,* later becoming the drama critic.